McBEin

A DIVINE
OPERATIONAL
GROUP STORY

DM GAITHER

PAGE PUBLISHING
Conneaut Lake, PA

First originally published by Page Publishing 2022

ISBN 979-8-88654-338-4 (pbk)
ISBN 979-8-88654-340-7 (digital)

Printed in the United States of America

Dedicated to all my Friends and Family for their continued support.

A Special Thank you to:

Pamela Burton
Alicia Mitchell
Stephen Paul
Angelo Miller

CONTENTS

CHAPTER 1

NIGHTMARE

It's that moment before you completely wake that anything is possible. Our minds will let us be anything, from rock stars to astronauts. Slowly reality starts to set in and bring us back to the real world. In McBeth's case, it was the searing pain in her shoulder that brought her back from a field full of butterflies as a child that she used to run through.

Her training took over, and she knew to listen to the room before opening her eyes in case she wasn't alone. Not hearing any movement, she slowly opened one eye then the other. She wasn't alone, but she was the only one awake or conscious. On her left was Mark Grimm, aka Reaper, and Thomas Irby. On her right were Rick Baylor, Wayne Rogers, and Dewayne Martin. All were still and not moving. All six had their hands tied to ends of a three-foot piece of pipe that was suspended in the air by a large chain; the chain was draped through a large pulley connected to an I beam that ran the distance across the room. Their captives could pull on the other end of the chain and easily lift an individual off the ground. All the chains were lowered enough that each prisoner could rest on their knees but could go no lower.

The room appeared be a bunker of some sort. It had concrete floors, walls, and ceiling. Its old florescent lights buzzed behind the rusted wire cage they were hidden behind. One grey metal chair was the only furniture in the room. A large black metal door with a small, five-inch window was the only entrance/exit in the room. The odors of sweat, urine, and blood permeated throughout the room. There were several blood spots on the walls from previous inhabitants of the room.

Seeing they were alone, McBeth whispered to Reaper, who was the closest to her.

"You awake?" she whispered.

"No," he said, opening his eyes to glance at her with a weary smile.

There was no telling how long they had been in the room. With no windows, it was easy to lose track. They knew they had been there long enough for their captors to question and beat them at least twice. All except McBeth, and that worried her. She wondered why she had been questioned, but no one had laid a hand on her. Meanwhile, the other men had been smacked around pretty good.

McBeth looked to her other side at Baylor; he wasn't moving and had a good amount of dried blood on his forehead.

"Baylor, you still with me?" she asked with no response.

On the other side of Baylor was Rogers. He spoke up, "He's been out for a while. He took a good beating last go-around."

McBeth tried again to wake Baylor.

"Baylor, wake your ass up right now," she said, trying to provoke a response. She would have kicked him in the groin, but she couldn't reach that far.

Baylor barely cracked open one eye and said, "Are we home yet, Mom?" He forced a slight grin as he said it.

McBeth knew Baylor was one tough soldier, but she worried about the injuries he had sustained.

Outside the door, they could hear footsteps and keys rattling in the door lock. The door started to open, and everyone closed their eyes and pretended to still be asleep. They could hear the door open then close. The captors locked the door, but they all knew the captors were in the room. As the captors made their way deeper into the cell, they whispered to each other.

"I'll put the gag in her mouth, and you keep watch at the door," said one of the captors.

"No, I get her first. We had a deal," said the other captor.

2

"Fine, you go first, then my turn, but we have to be quick and keep her quiet," he replied.

Any female but McBeth would have been quivering, but she held her breath and tensed her body.

The first captor, a small man with graying hair, eased toward McBeth, almost tiptoeing, not to wake the others. Just as he was about to reach around her face to tie an old dirty rag across her mouth, she opened her eyes.

"What are you doing?" she said in a loud voice that startled her captor.

"Shut her up," said the other captor, looking nervously through the small window in the door. This captor might have been larger, but his hunched frame and snarling mouth revealed he was just as much a coward as his buddy.

The man shoved the rag in her mouth to keep her quiet. McBeth gagged at the dirty rag and kicked her feet. She swung her arms that were suspended above her head.

"You better hold her still, or they will come and kill us both for messing with her."

One of the captors bent closer toward McBeth; the stench of his breath close to her face. She could see the lust in his eyes had clouded his reason. His breathing was heavy and deep as he prepared to loosen his belt.

McBeth understood that the captors thought she was the weakest link. *Just let them get close enough*, she thought, *and I will show them*. She jerked her lower body and prepared to launch a kick at her captor's midsection. They might think she was unable to defend herself, but her legs were free, and that meant she had a weapon at her disposal.

Just as McBeth prepared to kick, the Reaper yelled, "Get your hands off of her, you sick bastards!"

The smaller captor stepped away from McBeth and struck Reaper with a wooden baton, knocking him out. The taller captor saw this as his opportunity. He rushed from his post at the window and ran over to McBeth and started grabbing at her belt. The second man joined him in the assault. McBeth was kicking and fighting off the two men. She landed several kicks on the two assailants until one of them got a little smarter and grabbed her legs.

"Let her go, you bastards!" the other prisoners had long given up pretending to be asleep and were yelling and making all the noise they could. They knew their only hope to help McBeth was to gain the attention of the other captors.

"I've got her legs. When I let go, we will quickly jerk down her pants." The two men were in a frenzy to get her pants off. However, one would tug one way and the other the opposite, almost counteracting the other's action.

"You get her pants, and I'll raise her top," said the one captor. "If she doesn't stop fighting us, we can just knock her out. We don't need her awake."

The other nodded, and they started working together. They got as far as raising her shirt above her bra and unbuckling her pants when the metal door swung open.

"What are you doing?" said a large black man that ran in the room and temporarily blocked out the entire doorway.

Both men stopped and turned around, and one man said, "She didn't look like she was breathing, so we were trying to help her." Both men timidly stepped back away from her like little kids who had got caught with their hands in the cookie jar.

"She probably can't breathe with this rag in her mouth," the newcomer said as he ripped it out of her mouth.

Immediately, McBeth took a big breath of somewhat fresh air and glared at the two captors.

The two backed away toward the door as if to make their escape. They were too late. The large black man pulled his pistol and shot one of the captors in the head and pointed his gun at the second.

"Clean up this mess, and I'm going to make it your responsibility to care for her from now on," he said. "And you had better keep your hands and other parts of your anatomy to yourself."

The shaking man reached down and grabbed his buddy's feet and dragged him out of the room.

Once the body was gone, the newcomer turned to face his captives. "Now that we are all awake, let's get back to the questioning."

He walked over to Martin and Rogers. Just to be playful, he jerked on the chains restraining them. Then he looked at both men and said, "We are going to play a game. Do you guys like games?"

Neither man responded. None of the prisoners had said one word to the captors the entire time.

"I'm going to ask a question, and if you don't answer, I'm going to hit the other man." Looking at Martin, he said, "What is your name?"

Martin didn't answer, and the man struck Rogers in the face. A red crease streaked the cheek bone from where he made contact. He then asked Rogers the same question.

"What is your name?" he said to Rogers, who didn't answer.

The man stepped over and struck Martin and said, "It's just a simple question. Here, I'll start. My name is Apollo. See how easy that was."

He asked the men again the same question but got the same results. He walked over to McBeth and pulled down her shirt and re-buckled her pants.

"You owe me. At least tell me your name," he asked. Instead of answering, McBeth just slowly shook her head from side to side.

"Okay. I was trying to be nice, but maybe with a little more softening up, you will be more talkative. If you don't have anything to eat for a while, I bet you will be eager to answer my questions," Apollo said as he walked out of the room.

The door closed with a frustrated thud. Then the lights started flashing from strobe lights in the corners, and loud music began to blare into the room.

"You okay?" asked Reaper to McBeth.

"Yeah. I've had worse first dates," she replied.

CHAPTER 2

WHITE HOUSE

Rebolini's black Chrysler 300 pulled up in front of the main office. The Divine Group had purchased a partial of land the government sold at one of the public auctions. The entire facility consisted of four major buildings and several small structures that previously served as maintenance buildings.

The main office was the smallest of the four buildings but was the tallest at three stories. The main floor consists of a large foyer, reception area, and meeting rooms. The second floor was where the groups established a command center that was maintained by Jason "JJ" Jones, the resident computer geek. JJ also used space on the second floor for forensic evaluation and record keeping. The third floor was where the corporate offices were located. Cap, Smitty, and Stevens had their offices there. A fourth main office was used by Rebolini, when he wasn't at his downtown Washington, D.C., office.

The other main buildings were used for vehicle maintenance, training, and temporary housing.

Rebolini entered the main building to find Callie sitting behind the reception desk. All members of the team had several job functions, and this week, it was Callie's turn to man the front door. Rebolini knew she was more than just a good-looking woman behind the desk. He knew, if needed, she could remove any unwanted person without needing security's assistance.

"Good morning, Colonel," said Callie to the approaching gentleman.

"Good morning, Callie. How have you been doing?" he asked.

"Very well, Colonel," she said.

"Is the boss in his office?" he asked.

"No, sir. He's out walking Doodle, checking the grounds," she responded.

Doodle was Cap's pet dog and sidekick. He rescued her about a year earlier, and she had been a staple at the office ever since. But to hear it, Cap would say she rescued him. They were inseparable unless Cap was on a job.

"He sure loves to check the grounds and walk that dog," said Rebolini with a chuckle.

"I'm going to head up to the office to make a couple calls. When he gets back, will you tell him to stop in and see me, please," he added.

"Yes sir, Colonel, I will make sure he knows," she said.

Rebolini entered the elevator and disappeared behind the closing doors.

A few minutes later, Cap and Doodle returned from their walk.

As he approached Callie, Doodle ran to her side, wagging her tale. Callie and the others kept snacks for her at the desk. Callie opened the drawer and got her a couple.

"Now, were you a good girl?" she asked.

Doodle responded by sitting and wagging her tail. She received the snacks as a reward, along with a good ear-scratching.

"Cap, the colonel is in his office and wanted me to tell you to swing by when you got back," she said.

"Okay, thanks. Did he say what was up?" Cap asked.

"No, sir. He seemed calm and in a good mood, but you know the colonel," she said with a smile.

"True," responded Cap as he called for Doodle to join him in the elevator.

The elevator opened, and Doodle ran for Cap's office. It was nap time for her after her big walk.

Cap went to Rebolini's office. Stopping at the open door, he knocked before entering.

"Come on in, Cap," said the colonel.

Cap walked in and took a seat across the desk from Rebolini.

"So what brings you out to the sticks this early on a Monday morning?" asked Cap, getting straight to the point.

"We need to take a little ride and talk to someone," he said very cryptically.

"How prepared do I need to be for this little ride?" asked Cap.

"Leave-your-guns-and-put-on-a-suitcoat kind of prepared," responded Rebolini.

This can't be good, thought Cap.

"When do we need to go?" he asked.

"I left my car running at the front door," said Rebolini.

"Okay, let me make one call, grab my jacket, and I'll be ready," said Cap, leaving Rebolini's office and walking toward his.

In his office, he sat at his desk and removed his firearm, locking it in a secured drawer of his desk. He pulled out his cell phone and looked at his message. The only one he had was the one he received the night before from Smitty, reminding him they still needed to have a conversation. Smitty was referring to the information the terrorist Abid Yassin had given him in New York during their last "exercise." After the team cleared their name, they all went separate ways for a few weeks to get their heads back in the game. Plus, no new work had come across the board for them. He dialed Smitty's number and waited. No answer, so he left a message.

"Smitty, it's Cap. Give me a call when you get this," he said while picking up his jacket off the chairback.

After the phone beeped, he put it back in his pocket and left the office. Doodle was already asleep on her mat.

"Ready when you are, Colonel," he said, poking his head in Rebolini's office.

Rebolini just stood and met him at the door. They entered the elevator and headed down to the main floor.

"Callie, I'll be with the colonel for a little while. If Smitty calls, tell him the colonel dragged me away, and I will call him back as soon as possible," Cap said to Callie as the two men walked toward the door.

"Great seeing you, young lady," Rebolini said to Callie as he waved and walked out the door.

The two men got into the black sedan, with Rebolini driving.

"So can you tell me now where we are going?" said Cap. He knew from experience that something had to be up for Rebolini to insist suitcoat attire.

"Just sit back and relax. We have a forty-five-minute drive, and I'll let you wonder a little bit longer," said Rebolini.

Cap continued to ask the colonel, but he always got the same answer.

"You'll know soon enough" was the reply.

Cap knew they were going someplace in Washington but wasn't sure if it was CIA, FBI, DOJ, or maybe the Pentagon. However, when the vehicle rolled up to the east entrance to the White House, he was surprised.

"Are you kidding me?" asked Cap.

"Nope. Your presence has been requested, and I know how you feel about coming here," said Rebolini.

"Yeah, no way in hell would I have gotten in this car if I knew you were bringing me here. I told you three years ago, I would never set foot in this place, and now you have me hostage," said Cap angrily.

"That was the previous regime. Things are different now," said Rebolini.

"I doubt that," said Cap with his arms crossed like a little kid, knowing it was too late to turn back now.

The vehicle stopped at the side entrance, where two dark-suited men stood waiting. Rebolini got out of the car and talked to the men. One of the men opened the door for Cap.

"Sir, will you please follow me. I need you to wear this badge the entire time you are here at the White House."

Cap nodded and took the badge, pinned it to his coat, and followed the other three men into the building.

They walked past several offices and finally were led to a small sitting room. The room was decorated with antiques, most likely gifts to previous administrations. Furniture consisted of two leather couches facing each other and a small table in between. (*No magazines*, noted Cap.)

After a few minutes, the door opened, and a dark-suited man said, "They will see you now."

They! Who the hell are they? Cap thought but followed Rebolini and the man out of the room.

"Holy crap," Cap said under his breath. *Am I really being escorted into the President's Oval Office?* he said to himself. All the times before he had been at the White House, he was ushered into a small corner office and only spoke to aids of aides. This was the real deal, he thought.

"Good morning, Colonel," said the voice from behind the big desk. It was President Campbell herself.

Rebolini nudged Cap.

"Good morning, Madam President," said Cap. He thought the president was speaking to Rebolini.

"I apologize for saying colonel. Your men affectionately call you Cap. Is that correct?" she said.

"Yes, ma'am. That is correct," responded Cap. He should have thought that she would know about him prior to meeting with him.

"Would you gentleman please have a seat," she said, pointing to the chairs in the middle of the room.

They both sat down, and she came from behind her desk and joined them.

President Campbell was the first US female president. She was prior military, even if it was the Coast Guard. She served two terms as US senator for Georgia and was appointed by the previous administration to the Office of Judge Advocate General with the DOD. Her run for president was monumental, and her fundamental beliefs in our country's national security won her the election.

"Gentlemen, I have brought you here under false pretenses," she said.

Rebolini looked stunned; he thought they were there to brief the president about the device they found in Berlin. Cap wasn't surprised they were tricked.

"In a couple minutes, we are going into a command center where top brass is running around like chickens with their heads cut off, trying to defuse an international incident," she said.

"How does that involve us?" asked Cap.

"Well, it does, and it doesn't," she said, doing the DC sidestep.

"Yeah, things have really changed around here," said Cap, looking at Rebolini.

"Okay. Tell us the part that does," said Rebolini.

"Master Sergeant McKenzie Anderson," she said, looking straight at Cap.

Cap looked back at the president and said, "What is going on, and is she okay?"

"We know very little," she said as Cap rolled his eyes.

"What we have pieced together is that she and a small force of soldiers infiltrated a group of mercenaries in Romania and have been captured." With that said, she waited for a reaction.

Cap and Rebolini looked puzzled at each other.

"Do either of you have any information or idea why she would be in Romania?" asked the president.

"No," said Rebolini.

"Me neither," said Cap.

"When was the last time you saw her?" she asked.

Rebolini spoke up, "I last saw her four weeks ago when she flew back on our jet from overseas."

"What about you?" The president turned her steely gaze toward Cap.

"It's been a week since I saw her, but I spoke to her on the phone last Thursday," he replied.

"It seems on Friday (three days ago) she and five other men invaded Romania. And we have no idea why," she said as she turned to walk toward a far wall.

"What are we doing to get her, I mean, them back?" said Cap as edged closer to the president. His movements were mirrored by the Secret Service. The president waved back the Secret Service.

"Nothing," said the president. She approached Cap, and for a few minutes, a look of pure concern softened her eyes.

"As far as we know, the captors haven't officially been identified as US soldiers or citizens," she said.

"So we do nothing," Cap said as he again leaned toward the president. Rebolini caught his arm and pulled him back down.

"I don't like it any better than you do," she said, trying to calm Cap down. Almost without thinking, she rubbed her forehead and began to reach out toward the distraught man. But thinking better of it, she straightened her posture.

"Let's go in the command center and see what news we have. I remind you that you are a guest in my house, and I expect you to keep a calm head," she said, scolding Cap. Without waiting for a response, she began to move.

The two men followed her to section of the wall that didn't look like a doorway, but she pushed down on the trim, and a door opened. Two guards were standing at attention outside the door. They led the president down the hallway followed by Cap and Rebolini. Two other armed guards had fallen into the procession. They walked to another large double door that was guarded by two more armed guards. The guards leading their parade snapped to attention beside the door guards. The one guard closest to the door opened the door for the president. He stopped Cap and Rebolini as they entered to see if they were wearing their magic badges. They were, so they were allowed to follow the president. The room was full of people: soldiers, civilians, and others in between.

The president motioned for Cap and Rebolini to sit in chairs situated behind other chairs that encircled a great table. Those seats were reserved for D.C. *who's who* among military geniuses.

"What's the update, General?" asked the president as she sat in the chair at the head of the chair.

"We were able to confirm that Sergeant Anderson and two of her soldiers took a thirty-day leave of absence to conduct personal business," said the general.

"Didn't that seem strange to her command for the three of them to ask for the same thing at the same time?" asked the president.

"Yes, ma'am, it did raise questions, but evidently, the three were able to convince their commander to approve the leaves," he responded.

"I want to see the papers," she replied. "What else?"

"The other two men seem to be retired military," said the general.

Cap and Rebolini both started to wonder about the guys. *Maybe that's why he couldn't contact Smitty*, thought Cap.

"A Mark Grimm and Deshawn Martin," said the general.

Both men inhaled deep breaths. "Excuse me, General, did you say Mark Grimm?" asked Rebolini.

"Yes, Colonel. We were able to determine he joined the group soon after he arrived in Bucharest, Romania," replied the general. With that said, the general indicated the wall behind him. Multiple screens filled this wall, and on one of the oversized TV screens, the individual pictures of the team from video footage alongside their official US photo were displayed. They obviously had the right people.

"Our intelligence officers there were able to track their moves up until twelve hours before the news was leaked of the invasion," said the general.

"What else do we know, General? Do we know where they are and if they are still alive?" asked the president.

"Madam President, we are tiptoeing around, trying to get info. The last thing we need is the Romanian government to take the stance we sent these troops into their country," said the general,

"So what are we going to do? Just leave them and hope the Romanians release them out of the goodness of their hearts?" Cap blurted out.

"Mr. Rodgers, you are here as a courtesy, but the length of time you stay will be determined by how long you can keep your mouth shut," reprimanded the president.

Cap nodded, and his motion of locking his mouth and tossing away the key made the president smile.

"Glad we are on the same page," she said to him. Turning away from Cap, she redirected her attention to the man beside her. "Continue, General."

"We are working some back-room deals, trying to get more info on the team, but right now we are in a sit and wait mode. At least we aren't getting any heat from the Romanian government," said the general.

The general turned his attention away from the president, who was looking at Cap and Rebolini. She pointed to the two men.

"Okay, you two come with me." She once more turned to the general.

"General, I expect to be kept up to the second of what's going on."

The entire table snapped to attention as the president stood up.

"Yes, Madam President, I will update you every thirty minutes or as the information comes in," he replied.

"Thank you, General," she said as the group left the office.

Cap and Rebolini followed the president back to the Oval Office. Once there, she excused the escort, and it was just the three of them in the room.

"I don't have to tell you how important it is that we avoid an international incident with Romania," said the president.

"May I speak freely?" asked Cap.

The president studied Cap's face for a few minutes before responding. "Yes, please do."

"If you or any other of the fine officers in that room think I'm going to sit by and let members of my team rot in a Romanian prison or worse, you are crazy," said Cap, with Rebolini tugging on his coat sleeve.

"Actually, I'm counting on you not standing by," said the president, causing Cap and Rebolini to freeze for a second.

"I just need to know that you will get our people out without causing World War III." She looked at both of the men and waited a few minutes before adding in a tone dripping with sarcasm, "Surely, you didn't think I would invite you here just to tell you that your friends were captives in a foreign country. Surely, you must realize I am fully aware of your modus operandi and would never have dreamed you would sit this one out. Surely, you don't consider me a fool. I invited you here, so you would see the potential seriousness of this situation and use all the stealth you possess to get your friends out of this situation."

The two men stood silent until Rebolini replied, "I have several contacts in the area and might be able to get additional information."

Cap interjected, "I will get my team together and…" That was as far as Cap got when the president stopped him.

"I don't think I need to know any more, Mr. Rodgers. Just be safe and know if you get caught, you suffer the same fate as your friends. We won't be coming after you," she said, then added, "Don't get caught."

"I understand, Madam President," said Cap, keeping it short.

"Here's all I can give you, and it's off the record," she said as she handed him a folded piece of paper.

Cap took it and put it in his pocket without peeking. He and Rebolini turned away from the president and began walking through the corridors that separated the president from the other peons working in D.C. It didn't take long before both Cap and Rebolini were outside. The fresh air seemed antithetical to the stale air inside the White House, and he breathed deeply for the first time since arriving at the White House.

When the two men got in their car, Rebolini was the first to speak. "Did you know anything about this?"

"No," said Cap.

"What the hell were they up to?" he continued.

Cap pulled out his cell phone and called the Office. Callie answered on the other end.

"Callie, I need you to call the team and have them all report to the command center at 1500 hours. tomorrow." Without waiting on a response, Cap hung up.

"Let's give McBeth's Commander a visit. I know him," said Rebolini as the men sped off.

CHAPTER 3

APOLLO HOUSE

"We have to get out of here," said McBeth to Baylor.

"I don't know. I kind of like the music," she said with a slight smile. From the look on her face, Baylor knew McBeth was up to something.

"What's your plan?" he continued.

"One of us has to get out of these chains before we can do anything."

"Yes, but they aren't moving us to interrogate us. So it seems as if we are stuck here," he added. Just to add proof to his statement, he rattled his chains. The muscles in his arms flexed as a cramp caused him to grimace in pain. Although McBeth noticed the grimace, she wouldn't have seen it unless she had been closely studying Baylor's face. He was adept at hiding pain.

"Maybe we should start talking, but ask to do it in public," she said. "That way, they have to let us outside, and that improves our chances of escaping."

"Who goes first?" he asked.

"Let me go first, and if I get the chance, I'll make a move. If not, then we keep trying until we see our opening," said Reaper from her other side.

"Okay," she replied. Of all of them, Reaper would have the greatest chance of success. Not only was he strong, he was shrewd, and if anyone of them had the ability to talk himself out of a tough spot, it was Reaper.

Reaper grinned and began yelling, "I can't take this damn music anymore. I'll talk."

The music cut off immediately, although it took a few minutes before anyone entered the room. It was Apollo and two other guards.

"Who's the smart one that decided to speak up?" he said as he entered.

"Me. I'll tell you anything you want if you turn off that damn music," said Reaper.

"You better shut the fuck up," said Martin from the other end, playing along with the plan. The closest guard to him smacked him across the mouth and told him to shut up.

"Well, at least I have you guys talking," said Apollo with a big belly laugh. "What do you have for me?" said Apollo as he grabbed Reaper's face with his gorilla-sized hand.

"Can we speak in private?" he asked

"You too shy around your friends?" asked Apollo.

"It would be better if we spoke privately, you know, no distractions," he added.

Apollo looked at the other two captives. McBeth looked like she was ready to boil her friend alive if he muttered another word. Martin was still shouting for his friend to shut up.

Feeling like he had the upper hand, Apollo turned to one of the guards. "Get him down and bring him outside. Any tricks, shoot him in the head."

The guards lowered Reaper and unhooked the chain that connected to the pipe, keeping his hands tied. They had to help him walk since he had been tied up so long. The walked/dragged him down a short hallway into a small room. This room had windows, but all Reaper could see were trees and forest.

A few minutes later, the guards dragged Reaper back into the concrete room. His eyes were swollen, and he was bleeding from his mouth and nose.

"This is what happens to the next one that wants to waste my time," said Apollo

The guards reattached the chain to the pipe and raised Reaper until his toes were barely touching the floor. One punched him in the stomach right before turning to leave the room. When the metal door shut, Reaper looked at McBeth through bloody eyes and said, "Guess they didn't buy it that I was a Canadian here for bird-watching."

The captives started laughing. One guard banged on the door just as the strobe lights and the music resumed playing.

The guys spoke to each other, but it was mostly lipreading with the loud music playing. Also, they didn't know who might be listening.

Reaper said, "No opportunity. They handcuffed the pipe to a metal table."

"We need to try again," said McBeth. "But we will need to be crafty because they aren't so stupid to buy the same trick again."

"Let me try this time," said Baylor. "I think I can convince them to let me talk."

"No, that one guard is the same that came in here earlier and got interrupted. Maybe he will want round two," she said. "That gives me an opportunity to play along, and when I do, I am sure I can get him with his pants literally down again."

"Be careful. They don't have a problem smacking us around," said Baylor, winking at Reaper.

"Here we go," said McBeth as she started yelling for the guards.

"You guys play it up about me going into the other room," she added.

Again, the lights and music stopped, and the two guards returned. The metal door opened, and they heard Apollo from down the hallway. "Tell her I'm not wasting my time coming down there unless she has something good to tell me."

The first guard walked up in front of McBeth, and she looked past him to her suitor from earlier. She licked her lips and pushed out her chest.

"I'm so sore from hanging here, and I am so thirsty." She licked her lips again. "If you take me in the other room, I am sure we can come to some type of agreement for our mutual pleasure. Take me in the other room, and I'll give you what you want," she said with a sheepish smile.

The second guard pushed the first one to the side. He slid his hand down McBeth's arm to her shoulders.

"And what is it I want from you?" he said.

"Take your hands off her," said Baylor.

"Don't go with him. You know what he wants," said Reaper.

McBeth refused to look at Reaper; instead, she looked at the two guards. "These guys won't shut up, and if you try to take me in here, their yelling will alert Apollo. You don't want that, do you? You saw what he did do your friend, didn't you? Just take me in the other room and give me something to eat. Then I will make sure you two won't regret it."

The one guard started to say something, but McBeth had the guard closest to her too excited to listen or care. He motioned for the other guard to lower the chain so he could unhook the pipe. McBeth was already steadying herself when the guard unhooked the chain. With one motion, she drove the pipe down on the guard's chin, breaking his jaw. He fell to the ground, clinching his mangled face. The second guard ran toward her, but she moved quickly to close the space between them and thrusted the pipe upward, striking the guard's nose and driving it up into his brain. He stood stunned for a minute and then fell over his buddy. McBeth's hand still tied, she pulled the guard's Russian-made Kizlyar knife out of its sleeve and drove it through the first wounded guard's ear. She then pulled the knife from his brain and proceeded to cut one of Baylor's hands free. He took the knife from her and freed his other hand. Once free, he cut McBeth's hands free.

"Grab the other knife and cut the other's free," she said, dragging the bodies away from the partially open door.

Baylor cut the others free, and they all gathered behind the metal door.

"There are three doors before you get to the one that I was in," said Reaper.

"One was closed, the second was a bathroom, and the third was a bedroom with four beds," he continued to report.

"There are two more doors down the hallway, but I have no clue what is behind them. One must be the exit," he added.

The team removed the two knives and two wooden batons the guards had. No firearms. Hoping Apollo was the only other person in the building, they made their move. Silently they made their way down the hallway, past the closed door, restroom, and pausing at the bedroom. Baylor peeked in and saw Apollo sitting at a small table, writing on a tablet. Turning to McBeth, Baylor motioned he was going in and made the motion of slicing his finger across his throat. McBeth grabbed his arm.

"We may need a hostage," she whispered, and Baylor nodded.

Baylor slipped into the room and silently slipped up on Apollo. He never knew Baylor was there until the knife slightly cut his neck when he applied pressure.

"Think before you speak or move too fast, big boy," said Baylor in Apollo's ear. "My arms are a little tired, so don't test me," he said as he let the knife move a little, causing a small trickle of blood run down his neck.

"You will never get out of here alive," said Apollo slowly.

"Maybe we won't make it, but I promise, you will never see us die," said Baylor, twisting the knife and forcing Apollo to stand. The two men walked to the door and out into the hallway.

"Which way is out?" he asked Apollo.

"That door leads out, but you will never make it. I have guards everywhere," he added.

"Well, for your sake, you better hope your guards want to see you live because they make one move toward us, and you are history, my friend," said Baylor as he led the group to the exit. At the door, Baylor said, "Open the door slowly, but don't step out until I tell you to."

Reaper looked outside. "There is a tree line to our right, shouldn't be more than a hundred feet."

Apollo opened the door and stood there, just as instructed. There were a couple guards, but no one noticed the large man in the doorway.

"Okay, let's go," said Baylor, pushing Apollo through the doorway. The team moved to the right side and started down the side of the building. As they turned the corner, they were met by a dozen armed guards.

"Good morning, Lance Corporal Richard Baylor," said one of the men who seemed to command the others. "Let Apollo go, and we will not shoot any of you."

The guys were shocked to see the squad waiting for them but more concerned the man knew Baylor's rank and full name.

"I would do as he says," spoke Apollo.

Baylor looked back at McBeth, and she nodded for him to comply. Baylor took the knife off Apollo's throat and dropped it to the ground. Apollo stepped away, wiping the blood from his throat. He turned and punched Baylor in the face, knocking him down to one knee.

"You're lucky you belong to someone else. If not, I would kill you right here," Apollo said, leaning over a kneeling Baylor. He then stood and walked over to stand beside the man.

McBeth looked at the man for a long minute and then said, "I know you. You're Abid Yassin."

The group looked at the man as he spoke. "Yes, I am, and I'm here for my pound of flesh."

By this point, a group of Apollo's men had arrived on the scene.

"Take them back to holding and chain them up," said Apollo.

"Apollo, we need to talk about them," said Yassin.

"Let me get them secured, and we can speak, but like I told you on the phone, they are already spoken for," said Apollo.

The guards took the team back into the concrete room and placed them back in chains. They removed the two dead bodies as they left.

"What the hell is Yassin doing here?" asked Reaper.

"And what does he mean by pound of flesh?" said Baylor.

"I'm more concerned with the 'they are already spoken for' comment Apollo made, to be honest," said McBeth.

Moments later, Apollo and Yassin entered the room.

"It looks like you guys will live to see another day. Well, at least as far as I'm concerned," said Yassin. "Apollo has informed me that he has already negotiated your sale, and you will be sent on your way. I will say I am disappointed, but my true prize is going to be your Malcolm Rodgers or Michael Smith. I can wait till I have that opportunity," he added.

"And now that I know all your names, I can get even more money from my buyers," said Apollo, saluting Yassin.

21

Yassin walked over to the first prisoner.

He pulled his Ka-Bar out of its sleeve. He tapped the first prisoner and said, "Corporal Thomas Irby." He then walked down the line, saying each person's name and tapping them on their foreheads.

"Corporal Richard Baylor, Sergeant McKenzie Anderson, PFC Wayne Rogers, PFC DeWayne Martin, and last but not least, my good friend, Retired Sergeant Mark Grimm. Now, why is a retired Army Ranger hanging out with all these Marines, I wonder?" he said, grabbing Reaper's face.

Reaper just looked him in the eye and said, "Go fuck yourself, you pig-humping bastard."

Yassin smiled and looked over at Apollo.

"Do not kill him, Yassin. I need him alive to get my money," said Apollo.

"*Alive* is a relative term," Yassin said, looking back in Reaper's eye. Then he thrust his knife into Reaper's thigh.

CHAPTER 4

History Lesson

Smitty arrived at the company just before noon. When he walked in, he spoke to Kylie at the front desk.

"Cap in his office," he said.

"Yes, sir, and good morning to you too," she replied.

"I'm sorry, Kylie, it's been a long week," he replied.

"No worries. I was just busting your balls," she said, never one to mince words.

Smitty just laughed and headed to the elevators. Moments later, the doors opened on the third floor. Smitty didn't even go in his office and headed straight to Cap's.

He knocked at the open door and popped his head in.

"Got a minute?" he asked Cap, who was sitting at his desk, looking at a stack of paper.

"Sure, Smitty, come on in," said Cap.

"Not sure if this is a good time, but we need to talk," said Smitty.

"I know we do. Close the door," said Cap.

Smitty turned around and shut the door then walked over to sit down in front of Cap.

"How do you want me to start?" asked Cap.

"How much of what Yassin said was true? Is Malcolm Rodgers your real name, and what's the deal with being a colonel?" he started.

Cap came out from behind his desk and sat next to Smitty.

"I should have had this conversation with you a long time ago. Let me start with a story, then I will answer those questions," said Cap. He leaned forward and began his tale.

"Several years ago, I decided to become a police officer in my small hometown. Through a series of events, I ended up working for a government task force and received a lot of government training. When the task force ended, I was asked to continue working for the government on special assignments. Some of the assignments were in country and some outside the country. I ran a task force that consists of specially trained individuals. I was then tasked with developing a training program for the program, which had grown from a small group to a much larger force. Unofficially, I was given the rank of colonel through the police department by request of the government. So to answer one question, yes, I was once considered a colonel. To answer the next question, everything I have, birth certificate, driver's license, and government clearance, is under the name Malcolm Rodgers. That is my name. But it's not the name I was born with and spent twenty-five years using. Legally, I changed the name when the task force was eliminated by the government. Some of the work we did made a lot of people nervous in other countries and ours. To protect my family and friends, I changed my name and walked away from that previous life. Rebolini was assigned by the government as part of an oversight committee and helped me," said Cap, pausing only to let Smitty speak.

"So Rebolini knew you changed your name and knows your past," asked Smitty.

"Yes, he was the one who recruited me," continued Cap.

"Why did the task force get 86'd?" asked Smitty.

"A couple of the operatives went rogue and started working for hire, and it caused a split in the organization. Rebolini and I were on one side and a man named Theodore Hedstein was on the other. For a couple years, it was like playing a hit man's game where winner lived and loser lost. Hedstein's followers took out most of the operatives still loyal to the government. It wasn't until Hedstein himself was eliminated that the fighting stopped. The government was scared that it would happen again and cancelled the program," added Cap. Seeming tired from the explanation, Cap stood up and walked over to the lone window in his office. He stared at the blue sky overhead for a few minutes before turning back to face Smitty.

"Good lord. Sounds like a bad TV series," said Smitty.

"Yea, but these guys really died," responded Cap.

"So what did you do after that?" asked Smitty.

"I still worked for the government, along with Rebolini. The government decided that they only wanted a small group to continue under a new assignment. Rebolini, two other guys, and myself were all that stayed. The other remaining members were given new identities and lives. Except those that went rogue with Hedstein. The ones that remained were imprisoned and charged with treason," Cap added to the story.

"Why did you get out, or did you?" asked Smitty.

Cap walked back toward Smitty and resumed sitting. He placed his hands on his knees and leaned forward.

"No, I'm out, and so is Rebolini. The two other guys I mentioned died in the line of duty. They were just forgotten as the machine rolled on. I knew if something happened to us while we were on assignment, the government wouldn't step in to save us. But these guys died saving dozens of US overseas personnel and didn't get as much as a thank you or a decent burial. The government just swept it under the rug since the problem they solved was caused by an arrogant politician trying to boost his possibility of higher political office. I went along reluctantly until that politician became president, and I heard all the bullshit lies he told," said Cap, clinching his teeth.

"President Campbell?" asked Smitty.

"No, the one before. So Rebolini and I walked. We pondered on starting this company but wanted to have the right people involved. You and I had met on a couple jobs, and when we heard you had left the military, well, the rest you know," said Cap. He leaned back in his chair.

"I see, but why the secrecy of your past?" asked Smitty. This time, he leaned forward.

"It's a combination of threats from other countries and the nasty little business with Hedstein. The government didn't want any connects with the old task force group."

"So are you going to tell me your real name?" asked Smitty.

"If it's that important you know it, yes, I will."

"You know, I think I'll pass for now about the name. You need to remain a little mysterious, even to me. It gives you character," said Smitty, patting Cap on the back.

"Do you think I need to tell the rest of the team?" asked Cap.

"There were others with me in NY when Yassin made his statements. I wonder where he got his information," said Smitty.

"Not sure about Yassin, but today, when we meet, I will think of something to say," said Cap.

"Speaking of today, what's up?" asked Smitty.

Cap brought Smitty up to speed on McBeth, Reaper, and the other teammates' situations. With that finished, the two left to join the others in the conference room on the second floor. It was almost 1500 hours, time for them to plan how to rescue the others.

Walking into the room followed by Smitty, Cap looked at the faces of his team. They were all loyal to the bone, and now each of them had a look of determination and consternation on their faces. He knew they all deserved to hear his story, but now wasn't the time. There were more important issues to discuss.

"Callie, is everyone here?" asked Cap.

"Reaper is the only person missing, and I couldn't get in touch with him. He's not answering his cell," she said.

"That's weird. That guy lives on that damn thing," said Bain, concerned.

"Guys, Reaper will not be here today. He's part of the situation I want to brief you on," said Cap. Immediately all eyes were on him, so he began to explain. "Yesterday Rebolini and I were briefed by the government that Reaper and a small team were missing in Romania," said Cap.

Everyone started looking around the room, visually questioning what the hell was Reaper was doing in Romania.

"Reaper evidently went with McBeth and a few of her friends to Romania to retrieve McBeth's niece," said Cap.

"The colonel and I met with her commanding officer yesterday. He advised us that McBeth and a couple of guys from her team asked for a thirty-day leave of absence to settle family issues. The commander first refused the request from three of his officers, but once McBeth explained the situation, he approved the leave," explained Cap.

"It seems McBeth's niece was taken along with four other girls while backpacking through Europe. I contacted McBeth's sister, and she says there has been no ransom request or any news other than they went missing. She says McBeth contacted someone she knew in Romania, and they advised her they had heard of the abduction but didn't have any further information," Cap added.

"What we've learned from the government is that they have been captured," said Rebolini.

"But it's all been unofficial. The Romanian government is yet to contact our state department about the incident," said Cap.

"Why doesn't our government contact them?" asked Michelena.

"They won't. They are afraid it will cause an international incident and political fallout," said Rebolini.

"That's bullshit," said Murph.

"I agree. But we have to be smart about what we do," added Cap.

"So we are going to get them?" asked Murph. He had been leaning against a wall, but now he stepped forward.

"You're damn right, we are," said Cap as he examined the look on everyone's faces. He knew he could depend on them to get the job done.

"Before we get started, I want to clear up a couple things. First, if you're in this room, I consider you family. Though there are secrets among families, there is one I want to clear up," added Cap.

Everyone in the room had heard of the statements the terrorist made in New York to the guys.

"My past came up during one of Abid Yassin's rants a few weeks ago in NY. He called me by name and said that I and my team were blindly following the desires of our government, that basically we are puppets to our government's capricious nature. When we started this business, one of the main things we decided was, we were going to follow our guidelines and not the desires of our prospective clients. That means if we thought their intentions or criteria were against what we believe in, we would not take them on as a client. It also means that if the job the government was asking us to do was against our beliefs, we would pass on that job as well. Even if it meant losing them as a client," said Cap to a silent room.

"None of us blindly go into any situation. We have been tricked and lied to, and in those situations, we walk or undo the work we have done," added Rebolini.

"I just want you to know that trust in this room is important. Not just yours to us but ours to you. So if you have any questions, let's get them out in the open," said Cap, preparing himself for the onslaught.

"Keep in mind, we all have a past, and sometimes things need to be kept there—in the past," said Smitty, who received a slight smile from Cap, who knew Smitty was helping resolve the team's issues.

"If no one will ask, I will. Cap, we don't care if you real name is Rodgers or not. We don't care if you're a colonel, captain or a brigadier general. But the pool is up to $1000 as to what your background is. Is it military, police, or a professor of history? Can you answer that that one question?" asked Murph.

"Murph, I am prior law enforcement and government contractor. I started as a police officer in a small town and, because of a series of events, became one of the first and definitely the youngest SWAT officers in my area," said Cap.

MK stood up and started dancing. "Pay up, you suckers. I told you he was SWAT," he said while holding his hand out to Kylie, who was keeper of the pot.

"Any more questions?" asked Cap, looking around the room. Seeing none, he continued, "Good. Let's get to work."

Cap designated several tasks concerning logistics and equipment out to the team. The rest went to pack their gear and prepare for the most important task of all: bringing home their family!

"Cap, do you have a minute?" asked Callie.

"Sure, what's up?" he responded.

"My uncle was SWAT, and he always told me it took a special breed to do what he did. He said most SWAT guys had a specific triggering event that made them choose the job. Is that true?" she asked.

Cap sat down at the large table and slid a seat out for Callie.

"I believe it's true. It was for me," he responded.

"What happened, if you don't mind me asking?" she asked.

"I don't mind, but it's a tough story."

Callie just settled back and prepared for the story.

"Like I said a few minutes ago, I was a young police officer in a small town. Figured I would work there for a few years and then maybe go to work for the state police—writing tickets to speeders, maybe a few small theft reports, just simple things. And it was that way for a few months. My town, like others, had their local trouble-makers. We all know who they are and what they are about. There was this one man that live in a secluded part of the area. Part of the town I worked for was very rural and open country. He would, time to time, get rip-roaring drunk and get into a fight and get arrested. He lived with his wife, son, and two daughters. The son was the youngest of the three kids. The man lost his job with a local company that decided to move their plant to Mexico. It caused the man to be very angry, which caused him to drink even more. Usually, he got in trouble in town, but it started affecting him at home. Over a period of time, we got several calls from his children informing us that he was fighting with his wife. Once he got arrested, but she bailed him out. Finally, we got the call he was shooting a gun in the house.

"Four police cars responded to the call. When we got there, we discovered that the man had shot his wife and son. He shot his young-est daughter, but she escaped while her mother fought off her dad. The oldest daughter wasn't at home, but we thought she was there, so we didn't rush the house. He claimed to have hostages, so we waited. None of us had received any formal training in these situations, and it was a mess on our end. But the higher-ranking officers had us wait to try and talk him out. After about five hours, a car pulled up with the oldest daughter. She was out with friends. We knew then that he didn't have any hostages, and we started going toward the house. We heard one gunshot as we kicked the door open. We found him dead upstairs in the bedroom. We found the young boy dead in the living with a gunshot to the head. We then found the mother in the kitchen. She had a gunshot wound to her stomach. She lived for a while, waiting to be rescued while we sat outside scared to go in. She died because she saved her daughter, and we were too uneducated to go in and save her. I'll never forget her face. She had a calm look on her face. I like to think it was she knew her daughters were safe, and she was going to see her son." Cap told the story with only the slightest quiver in his voice.

"I swore then that I would never be afraid to step into harm's way to save others in need. I know that sounds a little corny, but I was twenty and impressionable," he added.

"What happened to the youngest daughter that got shot? I know you said she was okay," asked Callie.

"She was only nicked on her shoulder. I went over to her sitting on the back of the ambulance. She was in obvious shock. I took a blanket from my patrol car and covered her shoulder," said Cap.

"Did she ever speak to you?" Callie asked.

"She looked at me with tears pouring down her face and said, 'What do I do now? I've lost everything.'"

"I didn't really know what to say, but I remembered what I had heard in school. *You have to keep hope alive. Hope that there are better days and better things to come. Hope is being able to see that there is a light despite all the darkness.* I told her she and her sister would be okay and that if ever she needed anything to call me. I found out the next week, she and her sister went to live with their aunt in Pittsburgh. They both adjusted to their losses and grew up to be very special individuals," continued Cap.

"After that, I took every SWAT class and attended every specialized school I could, and here I am today," he said.

They both stood, and Callie gave Cap a brotherly hug and thanked him for the story.

"I think those two girls would be proud of the man you've become," she said, walking out of the room.

Cap looked down at his wrist and removed his watch. There tattooed under his watch was the word *Hope*. And he thought to himself, *I hope they are!*

CHAPTER 5

COUNTESS OF VILLACH

After the company meeting, Cap went to Smitty's office.

"Not sure if it's a good time to start this, but I have the report back on the new guys you wanted me to check out," said Cap, handing a folder to Smitty.

"My friends in the Corp highly recommended him, and I didn't want some other place to snatch him up without you looking at him first," said Smitty.

"Well, his record speaks volumes, and he definitely made an impression during the interview," said Cap.

"Okay, I'll set it up to have Cooper come in," said Smitty.

"Now, what are we doing about Reaper?" he added.

"I think we need to send a recon team to Romania. but I don't want to cause any more waves with the guys being held there," said Cap.

"Any ideas how we could get in without raising any eyebrows or bringing any attention to ourselves?" asked Smitty to Cap, who was rubbing his chin in thought.

"As a matter of fact, I do have an idea, but I need to make a call first," said Cap, disappearing into the hallway.

A few minutes later, he returned grinning from ear to ear.

"I have us an in," said Cap, smiling. "But we have to detour through Austria."

"Austria?" questioned Smitty.

"Yep, and I'll need to take one guy and two of the girls," said Cap.

"Take Murph, Aliah, and Pyle with you. I'll stay here to get an insertion team ready for Romania," said Smitty.

Smitty picked up the company phone and called Callie.

"Callie, I need four first-class tickets to Austria for tomorrow morning. Let me know the itinerary as soon as you get it. Also, contact Murph, Aliah, and Pyle and have them report for briefing in two hours. Thank you."

"What are you guys going to do in Austria?" asked Smitty to Cap.

"We are going to see the countess Emilia from Villach and act as her private security for her trip to Romania," said Cap.

"I think you secretly love that woman," said Smitty with a smile.

"What's not to love? She's smart, a quick thinker, and loves playing these games. She's perfect," said Cap.

"And she's filthy rich. Don't forget that part," added Smitty.

Cap just laughed and headed back to his office to prepare for the recon briefing. Although uncertainty about what was happening to McBeth and the others was gnawing at his gut, he knew how to compartmentalize.

For now, he would focus all his energy on getting them out. Since he had several plans to make, he headed for his computer and began planning. It wasn't long before a couple hours had passed, and it was time to meet up with the others. This time, he met with the smaller group in a first-floor briefing room. He entered to see Murph, Aliah, Pyle, Smitty, and Callie sitting at the table.

"Guys, I'm here to brief you on our mission. Murph, Aliah, Pyle, and I will be traveling to Austria. In Austria we will pose as a private security team for the countess of Villach. We will accompany the countess Emilia on her diplomatic trip to Romania on a sightseeing trip. There we will split up and see if we can gather any intel on our guys held there. Colonel Stevens has provided us with a few trustworthy contacts," said Cap.

"Do we have any further information on our guys?" asked Murph.

"No. There's seems to be a blackout on any information about where they are being held," said Cap.

"I really thought by now the Romanian government would be crying to the UN that Americans have invaded their country," said Smitty.

"Me too, but as they say, no news is good news," said Cap.

"We will work in teams of two along with the countess. She understands we need to move around the city, so she has agreed to join up with a friend's charity in Romania. The local charity specializes in historical restoration, so we will use that as an excuse to tour some of the seedier parts, looking at the buildings," said Cap.

"Good idea," said Aliah.

"Not mine. It was the countess who came up with it," said a smiling Cap.

"You guys are going to love the countess," said Smitty.

Knowing where Smitty was going with that comment spurred Cap to interrupt.

"Callie, when are our flights?" asked Cap.

"I have you guys booked nonstop to Vienna, leaving at 1000 hours tomorrow. It's a ten-hour flight."

"Since we are flying commercial, what about weapons?" asked Pyle.

"We will get what we need in Austria. And since we are diplomatic security, we will be able to carry them to Romania," said Cap. "Smitty will get the QRT (quick response team) set up. Callie, you and Mich need to prep the plane for a flight to Romania. We will have more info on where your destination will be, but be ready." He ended his comments. "See you all here at 0730 hours to head to the airport."

Cap watched as his teammates, his friends, exited the room. Each of them had a proud bearing that announced their confidence, not arrogance. Arrogance, Cap knew, got you killed.

The rest of the day passed quickly for Cap. He had Rebolini reach out to their contact in the White House. President Campbell had told them she didn't want any problems; that didn't, however, mean that someone in the White House shouldn't know what Cap planned to do. Soon it was the next morning, and the team was on its way to Vienna, Austria.

Nine hours and forty-five minutes later, the wheels of the Boeing 777 touched down in Vienna. The group worked their way through customs and the baggage claim. As they exited the main terminal, a large black limo pulled up in front. The sunroof opened, and a familiar face appeared.

"You guys need a lift?" said the older woman.

Cap recognized the countess right away.

"Only if the bar is open," he said.

The countess raised a bottle of champagne and said, "My bar is always open. Get your good-looking butt in here."

The group laughed as the driver opened the door for the team.

"Great to see you, Countess," said Cap, kissing her cheek. She leaned in for Cap's kiss, evidently enjoying his attention.

"Now, who are these lovely ladies?" asked the countess.

"Countess Emilia of Villach, let me introduce you to Aliah Moon and Marie Pyle. And of course, you remember Murphy," said Cap as he pointed to his friends.

"Guys, I present the Countess of Villach, Ms. Emilia Von Dietrich," said Cap with a wave of his hand.

"I am honored to meet you, Countess. I have heard so much about you from Reaper, I mean Mark Grimm," said Aliah.

"How is my dance partner, such a fine young man?"

"He's one of the people we are looking for," said Cap.

The countess's eye opened a bit, and she said, "Well, we will find him. I promise." She leaned over to pat Aliah on the knee.

The limo headed east out of Vienna, headed for Salzburg. The passing panorama, even with all its beauty, was ignored as the occupants of the car discussed strategy.

"We have to fly all diplomatic flights out of Salzburg. Stupid, I know, when we were just at a perfectly good airport. But you know how inflexible bureaucrats are," said the countess.

"When do you plan to fly out?" asked Cap. He figured they might have to spend a few hours in Vienna, but no more.

"We are headed to the airport now. That young man needs our help, and I'm not wasting one minute," said the countess.

"We had planned to get some equipment before we left," added Cap as he checked his phone for incoming information.

"Oh, if you mean guns, open that black suitcase," said the countess.

Cap opened the case that was occupying the space next to the countess, and there were four Glock 30s and four 9mm Steyr machine guns. All had extra magazines and shoulder holsters.

"The best Austria has to offer," said the countess.

"I told you guys you were going to love her," said Cap as he passed out the weapons.

A few hours later, the limo pulled up to the private entrance to the Salzburg Airport. An elderly security guard came out to check the vehicle.

"Good evening, Countess. Late flight tonight?" he asked.

"Yes, Henry, we are going to Bucharest, Romania, for a charity event," she replied.

"Anything to declare before you leave," he asked.

"No, our machine guns are all on safety, so we should be good," said the countess to the laughter of the guard.

The limo entered the tarmac and drove up to the large jet.

"I thought we were flying as diplomats on a commercial flight," asked Murph.

"Don't be silly, young man. I don't do commercial anything," she said with an infectious laugh as she whipped her scarf around her neck. With nothing more to say, the group followed the countess as she boarded the plane. Within minutes, they were headed to Bucharest, Romania.

Although the countess was used to entertaining guests, this time she sensed the gravity of the situation and allowed the team members space to prepare and review their plans. Once they landed in Bucharest, they were met by security at the private terminal.

"We must check your plane and its passengers before you can exit the plane," said the airport security.

"We are a diplomatic envoy here from Austria with the countess of Villach," said the pilot to the guard.

"We do not have any information about this visit. Therefore, we must follow normal airport procedures," replied a guard.

There was no use try to hide the weapons; a normal search of the plane would find them, and that would make it worse.

"Oh great, now we have another group of armed Americans invading Romania," said Murph.

"Hold on a minute," said the countess as she made her way to the guard.

"My young man, you look like a bright fellow. Would you mind if we stepped outside to talk," she said to the guard.

"Ma'am, I'm not allowed to let you off the plane until we have searched the plane and all the passengers," said the guard.

The countess placed her hand on the center of the guard's chest and said, "I only need to make one phone call to clear this up. You can frisk me, and I promise not to run."

The countess gently pushed the guard backward as she pulled her phone from her coat pocket. She hit a couple buttons and spoke German to someone on the other end. She hung up and stopped on the stairs of the plane with the backpedaling guard.

"Someone will be calling you in a moment," she said to the guard.

On cue, the guard's radio went off. The voice on the other end told him the plane had diplomatic clearance and he better be on his best behavior with the countess. Having received his orders, the guard quickly changed his attitude.

"Welcome to Romania, Countess. Please let me escort you to your transportation," said the guard.

The countess just slightly bowed and reached out her arm for the guard to escort her to the arriving limo. The rest of the group, hearing they were clear, followed her lead and got into the limo. The guard stood and waved as the limo left the terminal.

"First stop is my friend's charity headquarters. He is very connected with the government and might have some information about our friends," she said.

"We don't want the government to know we are here," said Cap.

"He is very discreet and owes me. He won't say a word to them," she added.

The limo stopped at the restored historic landmark building used as the charity's headquarters. The group exited the limo and went inside. They were met by a tall, slender man in his late seventies.

"My friends, I would like to introduce Arthur Shuman, director of historical archives of Romania," said the countess.

Arthur snapped to a formal greeting, complete with a customary heel click of his feet.

"The pleasure is mine," said Arthur as he reached out to shake their hands.

"Arthur, is there a place we can talk in private?" asked the countess.

"Yes, follow me," he said as he turned briskly and started walking toward two large wooden ornate hand-carved doors.

The group entered, and Arthur closed the doors.

"Would anyone care for a cognac?" asked Arthur.

The group declined, but the countess looked at the team and shook her head.

"Yes, Arthur, we would all like a cognac," she said, almost scolding the team in the process.

Arthur motioned for the guys to sit and poured the drinks.

Drinks in hand, Arthur raised his glass.

"To friends, old and new," he said, and the group drank the shots.

Cap had an immediate flashback to drinking Grand Marnier with Donny in Myrtle Beach.

"Now, what can I do for you, my dear?" asked Arthur, sitting down next to the countess.

"Arthur, this is strictly confidential and has to stay between us. Do you understand?" asked the countess.

"Yes, I understand," said a puzzled Arthur. He leaned back in his seat and waited.

"Have you heard of any Americans being held by the government?" she asked.

"No, nothing like that at all, but I can make a few calls if you like," said Arthur.

"Only if it's someone you trust," said the countess.

"What is this all about?" he asked.

"A group came here looking for a missing girl and got mistaken as soldiers here on mission," she continued. "Seems they were captured and are being held somewhere in Romania."

"I will help as best I can, but if they were here against my country, I will not help you," said Arthur.

"Arthur, I promise, they are only here to find a little girl and have nothing to do with governments or politics," she added.

Arthur considered her comments. "I understand. Let me make a couple calls," he said, moving to his desk. It was a large oak desk with neatly piled folders and an antique phone. A high sheen reflected Arthur's reflection as he picked up the receiver. "This might take a few minutes, so feel free to look around. We have some of the best sculptors in the world in this building."

The guys left the room to let Arthur make his calls. It didn't take long before he had finished. By then, the team had returned to his office; they hadn't wanted to sightsee, so they had only ventured a few feet from Arthur's office. Cap had stayed right outside the door as he attempted to overhear what Arthur was saying. The countess might trust Arthur, but since Cap didn't know the man, he was reluctant to blindingly trust the countess's friend.

The door to Arthur's office opened, and he motioned the countess and her friends to rejoin him. "I've made a few calls, but it's late. I will probably hear back from them in the morning. Why don't you go get some rest, and we will start fresh in the morning?"

The group agreed and headed to the hotel.

Understanding that this might be the last chance for a good night's sleep, the team knew to take advantage of the opportunity. They were trained to sleep on demand, so they didn't find it difficult to go to sleep.

Early the next morning, they headed back to see Arthur. They arrived early, around 0800 hours. Even so, the building hummed with activity. Numerous individuals were busy bringing the old building to life. After a brief nod from the receptionist, they entered and went immediately to Arthur's office. He was sitting behind his heavy antique oak desk, talking on the phone. He hung up as the group walked in.

"Good morning, Arthur," said the countess.

"Good morning, everyone. I hope you got some rest," replied Arthur.

"Do you have any news for us?" replied the countess, getting straight to business.

"There is no record of any Americans or any foreign team being held by the government," answered Arthur.

"How can that be? I've seen satellite footage of the team being taken into custody," said Cap.

"All I can say is, the Romanian government is not involved in whatever you saw," said Arthur.

"What the hell is going on?" asked Murph.

"Wait, you said all you can say is, the government is not involved. If it's not the government, then who is it?" said Cap.

"I'm not sure if this is the case, but you said the team was here to get a missing girl. Did the girl go missing from here, or was she brought here after she went missing?" asked Arthur.

"Are you saying there's a nongovernment group that has the team that is connected to the missing girl?" asked Cap.

"I'm saying that's a possibility," continued Arthur.

"Human trafficking," said the countess. "It's becoming big business here in Europe."

"Oh Lord, those poor girls," said Aliah.

"It's not just girls. They are selling men, women, and children all over the world," said Arthur.

"Is there a group here in Bucharest involved in the business?" asked Cap.

"Let me make a few calls to find out, but we need to be careful. If they are here and we ask the wrong person, it could hurt your chances of finding your people alive. Most of my contacts are loyal, but there are those that take payoffs from these people to keep them from being discovered," said Arthur.

Arthur picked up his phone to make a couple calls. "I know you didn't take advantage of wondering about the building yesterday," he paused before continuing. "My people are quite loyal, and they told me you basically just stood outside my door in the hallway." Seeing that countess was about to intervene, he raised his slender hand and smiled at her. "I totally understand, but these phone calls are going to take me a few minutes, and some of the people I am calling trust me to keep their identities secret, so you can either sit outside in the lounging area or take advantage to view some remarkable artwork. Either way, you are going to have to wait for me to finish, so why not enjoy learning about Romania's history."

Understanding that Arthur was not going to bend, the countess led the team to the lounging area. "There is no need to offend Arthur," she stated.

Cap started to interrupt. "I get it, you don't have time to wander, but since I am your so-called host in this country, I am asking you to at least pretend to be civil."

With that said, the countess led the group to a bar sitting in the corner of the lounger. The countess sat down next to decanter filled with cognac and reached for a glass. Murph snapped into action and filled it for her. Cap pulled out his cell phone and called the office to check in. The girls set about looking at the paintings and sculptures. They paused only for a brief minute or two to snap a few selfies. Looking at the frivolity of their faces, it was hard to believe these two young ladies could turn stone-cold killers when needed.

Less than twenty minutes later, Arthur opened the door to his office. His silver hair looked disheveled as though he had been raking his hands through it. He motioned to the group, and they followed his lead and reentered his office.

"There is an organization that operates all over Europe and most of Asia that has a presence here in Romania. According to my source in Interpol, they move around and don't stay in one city too long," reported Arthur.

"Are they the ones that have our people?" asked Cap.

"He told me that they were here a few days ago, but he was not sure if they have moved on," answered Arthur. "He didn't say anything about them having your people, but they definitely were here."

"We need to go to the place where the satellite shows the team being caught," said Cap.

"You have to be careful going to some areas around here. They don't take well to strangers walking around, asking questions," said Arthur.

"We will be fine. Remember, we are here to help make their communities better," said the countess. "Everyone wants free money, so I think we can persuade the locals to listen." After saying this, the countess stood and walked over to Arthur. Taking both of his hands in hers, she squeezed. A smile spread across her face, and she bent to kiss Arthur's cheek. "Thank you, old friend. You have helped us so much."

Arthur returned the gesture and the smile. "Anytime, my dear. You know I would do anything you ask."

During this exchange, Cap and his team stood silent, but impatient. They understood that this intimate exchange hinted at a deep relationship between the two, but they also felt the pressure of time slipping away from them. While the countess and Arthur chatted and enjoyed themselves, McBeth and the others might be suffering.

As soon as the exchange ended, Cap reached out to take the countess by the arm. She turned to look at Cap and, seeing the expression on his face, knew it was time to leave. Without further discussion, the group exited the building and headed to the limo.

Once inside the car, Cap turned to his team members. "I have the last known coordinates. Let's see what's around there."

"Murph, if we get into any trouble, your only job is to protect the countess, copy," ordered Cap.

"Copy that," replied Murph.

After a few minutes ride, Cap spoke up, "Stop here!" He pointed to a vacant lot next to an old warehouse.

"Bet you a dollar they are in that warehouse," said Cap.

"Looks empty," said Aliah.

"Murph, stay here with the countess, and we will go check it out," said Cap.

Aliah, Pyle, and Cap checked their weapons and fast walked across the vacant lot to the warehouse entrance. The building was circled with a dilapidated wire fence, and it looked like no one had been there for years.

"New lock on the door," Aliah announced.

"Well, someone has been here," said Pyle.

"Check to see if there another entrance," Cap told the team and immediately split up to check around the warehouse.

"I got an unlocked door on my side," reported Pyle.

Aliah and Cap joined her at her discovery.

"Quietly," said Cap as he opened the door and eased into the building.

The warehouse must have been used as a mechanic shop. It was a single-story building made entirely of concrete. The team worked their way through the building, checking the rooms as they went.

"Smell that?" said Aliah.

"Yeah, you can't miss that smell," answered Cap.

The group pushed open a metal door to the last room at the end of the hall. Inside reeked of the metallic scent of old blood. On the walls were several splatters of dried blood. Overhead hung six chains that looked like they had been used to suspend something or someone.

"This is the place," said Aliah, looking down on the floor.

"How do you know?" asked Pyle, walking over to her.

Aliah just pointed to the blood writing on the floor. Someone had used their foot to write letters in blood. It said *DOG*.

"That has to be Reaper," said Cap. "We missed them," he continued, smacking his fist against the concrete wall.

"Let's get out of here," he added, and the team returned to the limo.

"Find anything?" asked the countess.

"This was the place, but they are gone. We must have missed them by hours," said Cap.

"Are you sure?" asked Murph.

Aliah showed Murph the picture from her cell.

"Dammit," snarled Murph. "What do we do now?"

"We head back to Arthur's to regroup," responded Cap as the limo sped out of the vacant lot.

Back at Arthur's office, Cap immediately called Rebolini.

"Colonel, I need some information. We believe that the team wasn't taken by the Romanian government but by a smuggling syndicate that specializes in human trafficking," informed Cap.

"That would answer a lot of questions why we haven't heard from the Romanians," said Rebolini.

"I need you to contact the general and see if he has any satellite surveillance for the last twenty-four hours. I'm looking for any truck movement at the following coordinates," said Cap, giving Rebolini the numbers.

"I'll call him right now," answered Rebolini, hanging up the phone.

"Now we wait. Arthur, do you have any local contacts that may know anything about this syndicate?" asked Cap.

"Yes, while you were gone, I made a couple calls, and I found out they have a local man that handles their business at the Grand Bizarre," responded Arthur.

"Grand Bizarre?" asked Murph.

"It's like a shopping mall and flea market combined," said the countess.

"You can buy anything there," said Arthur.

"Here, I have an old surveillance photo of the man sent to me from my friend," he added, showing the picture on his cell phone.

"Forward that to me, please," replied Cap.

"Smitty, take Pyle and go to the bizarre and get eyes on this man," continued Cap. He pointed to the picture of a forty-something man who had brown hair and brown eyes. He had the appearance of an individual who would easily fade into the background. However, Cap's team was trained in noticing even the slightest nuances of an individual's appearance, so they studied the picture for a few seconds until they felt confident that they would be able to pick out this man even from a crowd.

"I have a scooter you can use," said Arthur, retrieving a set of keys from his desk. "The bizarre is easy to find. Its directly in the center of town. The street outside of this runs into it."

Murph took the keys and followed by Pyle left the room. Once outside, they jumped on the scooter and headed to the bizarre.

"I hate waiting," said Aliah.

"Me too," responded Cap.

"Me too," added the countess, raising her glass for someone to fill.

Cap completed the task just as his phone rang.

"Are you near a computer?" Rebolini asked over the speaker phone.

Arthur pointed to his desk, and Cap responded, "Yes."

"Check your email. I've forwarded the information from the general. Looks like you guys may be right about the Romanian government not being involved," continued Rebolini as Cap logged onto this email.

Cap retrieved his messages and brought up the pictures.

"Looks like they are loading boxes onto the trucks," said Cap.

"Yes, and take a close look at those boxes. Do those look like air holes cut in them?" questioned Rebolini, knowing the answer.

"I count eight boxes," said Cap. "Do we have any pictures of where they took the boxes?" he continued.

"No, the satellite moved out of range just after these photos, but we do have a picture of a rather large man that seems to be the one giving orders," said Rebolini.

Cap brought up the final picture, which was a zoomed-in picture of a large black male.

"Do we know who he is?" asked Cap.

"Working on it, but the general said they ran him through facial recognition and came up empty," added Rebolini.

"Okay, thanks, Colonel. We will work on it on this end too. Would you mind updating Smitty?" asked Cap.

"He's sitting right here with me and is up to speed. Let us know if you find anything, and we will do the same," said Rebolini as he hung up the phone.

"We need to find this guy," said Cap as he pulled the photo from the printer and laid it on the desk.

Meanwhile, Murph and Pyle had arrived at the Grand Bizarre. It was jam-packed full of vendors of all sorts. It seemed to go on for blocks.

"We don't have the time to just sit and wait for this guy to show," said Murph.

"What do you suggest we do? We can't go asking, showing the picture around, and ask if anyone knows him," responded Pyle.

Murph pulled out his phone and called Cap.

"Cap, we need some help. There's too much area to cover, and it will take us forever," complained Murph.

"Arthur, does your contact have any info that could help us find this man?" asked Cap.

"Let me check. Hold on one minute," said Arthur.

"Hold on, Murph, he's making a call," conveyed Cap.

Arthur talked on the phone for a few minutes then hung up.

"My friend says to check the papanasi vendor near the antique store," said Arthur.

"What the hell is a papanasi?" asked Cap.

"It's like a fried donut stuffed with white cheese and usually topped with fruit compote," answered Arthur.

"Arthur said check with the guy selling fried donuts near the antique store," paraphrased Cap.

"I see an antique store and smell the donuts," said Pyle. "We must be close."

"Wait, don't hang up. When you get to the donut man, hand him the phone," said Cap.

They walked around for a minute and found the vendor Cap was describing. An elderly man was busy dipping batter in some really used frying oil. Murph walked up to the man and just reached out the phone.

"It's for you," he said.

The old man took the phone and spoke to Arthur on the other end. When he hung up, he reluctantly pointed to a café across the street.

"I'm guessing Arthur asked where we could find the guy," said Murph, on the phone with Cap.

"Yes, I heard him tell the man to point you in the right direction," answered Cap.

"Well, he literally did point to where we needed to go," said Murph.

"Keep me updated, and as soon as we hear back from Rebolini, we will join you," responded Cap.

Murph hung up the phone, and the two went to the café. They checked the inside and didn't see their guy. So they sat at a table facing the door and kept watch. They ordered a couple caffeine drinks and settled in. It didn't take long. The man they were looking for came out of an office in the back of the café and sat down at the bar. He ordered a drink and downed it quick. He ordered another but was met by another man before he could chug this one. The guys couldn't understand what they were talking about because they spoke Romanian to each other, but whatever it was, the new guy wasn't happy. Slamming his hand down hard, the bartender looked at him, only to get scolded in Romanian. Eventually, their guy was able to calm the new man down. The new guy stood, shook the guy's hand, and walked away. It appeared their guy was happy the new guy left. He downed his drink and started out of the café. The team followed the man down the street, past the bazaar, and into a small row of houses. Their guy went into the third one in the row. Murph took up a position in the back while Pyle watched the front.

Cap's phone rang. "Hello, Colonel. What did you find out?" asked Cap

"The man in the picture is known as *Apollo*," answered Rebolini. "He's a known mercenary and has been working throughout Europe and Asia for years. He was born in South Africa and trained with the South African Army and the Foreign Legion."

"Anything else?" asked Cap.

"We are working on trying to track the truck, but we have limited satellite coverage in that area," responded Rebolini.

"Let us know if you find anything, and thank you," said Cap as he hung up the phone.

Cap texted the picture to Murph's phone then called him.

"Murph, I sent you a picture and a name of the black man. Do you still have eyes on your guy?" asked Cap.

"He's in a house south of the bazaar. He went in about thirty minutes ago and hasn't come out. Not sure if he's alone, but no one has gone in since he entered," answered Murph.

"Cool. We are on our way. Time to pay the local rep a visit," said Cap.

Arthur drove Cap and Aliah to the area of the house; he knew the area. The two got out of the limo and walked the last part. As they approached, they saw Pyle across the street, sitting on a porch, reading a Romanian paper.

"I didn't know you could read Romanian," responded Aliah.

"She can't. The paper is upside down," said Cap with a smile.

Pyle looked at the paper and turned it upright.

"So which place are we looking at?" asked Cap.

"The third house from the end," she said as she looked in the direction of the house.

"Murph is set up out back, and no one has come nor gone while we've been here," she added.

"How do you want to play this?" asked Pyle.

Cap reached over and picked a potted plant from the patio and said, "Go pay your neighbor a visit."

"Who could resist two attractive women bearing gifts?" he stated.

"His wife," said Aliah.

"Girl, you got this. Just see if you can tell if he is alone. If he is, I need a sign to tell Murph to enter the rear of the house," he continued.

"If I start point down the street, he's alone," said Pyle.

"Okay. I'll have Murph standing by," said Cap.

The girls started for the house, and Cap called Murph to let him in on the plan. As the girls rang the doorbell, Murph moved into position to enter the house.

Aliah rang the bell, and an impatient Pyle knocked on the door. A couple seconds later, their guy opened the door and went straight into *I know this scene from Pornhub* mode. Leaning against the door frame, stroking his short beard, he smiled from ear to ear.

A couple of minutes later, Pyle was pointing down the road.

"Go Murph," ordered Cap over the phone.

Murph sprang into action. Silently he cut the screen and popped open the door lock. A couple seconds later, the man stood erect in the doorway and slowly disappeared into the house. Pyle looked at Cap and waved for him to join them. Cap ran across the street and in through the open door. Aliah closed it behind him. Murph called out from a room in the rear of the house. Murph walked into the kitchen, and there was their guy sitting in a chair with his hands already tied behind his back.

"Do you people know who I am?" said the captive.

"No, sir, would you mind telling us your name?" asked Cap in a tone that drenched with sarcasm.

"I'm not telling you shit, except you are all dead," the tied-up man responded. Even though he was tied up, he didn't look overly concerned.

"Listen, I don't have a lot of time, so I'm going to tell you how this goes," said Cap. "I'm going to ask you a question, and you are going to answer me. When we have what we came for, we will leave you alive. You won't tell anyone we were here because they will kill you for talking to us, so let's get started," he added.

"I'm not saying anything," said a defiant captive.

"I really hate this method, but it works too good, and right now, I don't have time to wait you out," said Cap, dragging his chair to the kitchen sink and turning on the water.

"When the sink gets full enough, I'm going to stick your face in it until you talk or drown. Do you understand me?" asked Cap.

"Fuck you and your CIA bullshit," said the captive.

"Okay," said Cap as he pressed the chair against the front of the sink cabinet and pivoted the chair upward, dipping the captive's head in the water.

"Cap, don't kill him. We need answers," said Murph.

"He can make the choice, talk or die. I don't have time to waste," said Cap with the thrashing man splashing the water all over the sink and Cap.

Cap could hear the man say, "I'll talk," under the water, so he sat the chair back on the floor.

The coughing man said, "Ask me your questions."

"What is your name, and do you know this man?" Cap asked, showing the man the picture.

"Yes," said the man. "And my name is Eurie."

"What is his name?" Cap asked, seeing if Eurie was going to lie to him.

"His name is Apollo, and he is one tough dude," answered Eurie.

"Good. Now, Eurie, what do you know about the people Apollo had in the warehouse?" asked Cap.

"I know he sold some and took some with him," said Eurie.

"Sold them," responded Cap.

"Yes, a girl went somewhere in China, and some men went to Africa. Mali if I'm not mistaken," said Eurie.

"Do you know where Apollo is now?" asked Cap.

Eurie hesitated, and Cap started to raise the chair.

"Stop. Apollo is in Constanta, on the coast of the Dead Sea," shouted Eurie.

"How did he move the people?" asked Cap.

"They were smuggled onto ships going across the Dead Sea," answered Eurie. "Then they were flown close to the final destination. The company has smuggling pipelines everywhere, even your United States," said Eurie.

Cap thought about flipping old Eurie up into the sink but stood by his word, and they left him unharmed as they left. They walked a few blocks and met up with Arthur in the limo and headed back to his office.

"So we need to get to Constanta as soon as possible," said Cap.

Arthur spoke up, "We have a tour bus that travels the historical sites all over Romania. Feel free to borrow it. If you get in trouble, I will report it stolen."

"How far away is Constanta?" asked Murph.

"About two hours' drive," replied Arthur.

The team returned to the office and talked to the countess.

"We are going to Constanta to talk with this Apollo. Not sure when we will be back, but most likely, we will be traveling fast. When you get the call, be ready to get your plane ready to take off," said Cap. Not waiting for the countess to answer, Cap turned to follow Arthur. They walked down the hallways decorated with ornate sculptures until they came to a door that led to the garage where the bus was kept. After opening the door, Arthur led them to the aging tour bus.

"She is old but runs like a top. Try to not get any bullet holes in her. It discourages the tourists," punned Arthur.

The team loaded up and headed for Constanta.

CHAPTER 6
CONSTANTA BEACH

The 1972 BredaMenarinibus had seen its tours around Romania, but it ran like a top. The Italians sure knew how to make a bus, but Arthur's people did a great job keeping the antique in good shape. Then again, restoring antiques was their business.

The old bus rocked back and forth, traveling the winding road from Bucharest to Constanta. Located on the west coast of the Black Sea, Constanta is one of the premiere beaches in Romania. The port is the largest on the Dead Sea, probably why Apollo and his crew used it to smuggle their goods to other countries. About a third of Europe drains into the Black Sea, making it easy for a smuggler to travel between locations.

Arthur had sent one of his people to drive the bus for the guys. He was a longtime trusted employee that knew the road well and the possible shortcuts if needed.

"How much longer?" asked Murph like an impatient child.

"About twenty minutes, if we don't hit traffic," responded the driver.

Murph turned to the guys and said, "Driver says twenty more minutes."

"How you want to play it?" Aliah asked Cap. She was sitting in the seat in front of him.

"We know what Apollo looks like, but I don't think we want to ask too many questions if this is his main port of smuggling," replied Cap. "He probably has the local government indebted to him. It's a large port, but I'm betting they stay in the lesser-used parts."

"Ask the driver which part of the port isn't used much," suggested Pyle.

Murph walked back to the driver.

"Hey, pal, I have a question. Arthur said you know a lot about the ports. Which one is used the least? We are trying to narrow down the possibilities to find this dude," said Murph, showing the driver the picture.

"That's a bad man," said the driver.

"You know of him?" asked Murph.

"Yes, people stay away from him and his men. Very bad men. Is that who you are going to Constanta to find?" asked the driver.

"He has our friends, and we have to find him. Do you know anything that will help us?" asked Murph.

"There is a local place that he and his men hang out. It is near the port, but I will not go there," said the driver, slowing the bus.

"You don't have to go there. Just get us close and point the way. We can meet you at a safe place when we return," reassured Murph.

The driver stepped back on the gas and nodded okay. "I will get you close, but not too close," he replied.

Murph returned to the guys and told them about the conversation he had with the driver.

"This Apollo has everyone scared of him and his men," said Murph.

"I'm sure it helps keeping people from cooperating with anyone trying to take him down," stated Aliah.

"Not going to help him today. He messed with the wrong people this time," said Cap as he loaded a magazine in his Steyr.

The driver drove the bus around the city blocks in Constanta, working his way to the port area. He pulled the bus into a market parking lot and stopped.

"This is as close as I will go," said the driver to the guys.

"How much further is the place you are talking about?" asked Murph.

"If you go down two blocks and turn right, the road will lead you directly into the port's main entrance. The building I told you the bad guys go to is one block down from the entrance. It's a water sports shop that rents scuba equipment," advised the driver.

"Anything else you can tell us?" asked Cap.

"Yes, don't go. Everyone around that place works for the same people Apollo does. None can be trusted, and they do not like outsiders poking their nose around their business," replied the driver.

"Then how do they expect to rent equipment if they don't like people coming in there?" asked Pyle.

"Because it's a front," answered Cap.

The driver nodded and said, "That gear has probably never left the building in five years."

The team gathered their equipment and started off the bus.

"We will meet you back here as soon as possible. Will you be okay waiting here?" asked Cap.

"I will drive around. They are used to seeing the tour bus on these streets. I will be close when you need me," replied the driver as he closed the doors and drove away.

"I'm worried our ride will not be around when we need it," said Murph.

"Arthur says he's trustworthy, and I don't think he would send just anyone on this trip. We are just going to have to trust Arthur's choice," responded Cap.

The guys went into the market and bought some water and a local map. Outside they opened the map and looked at the port section. Several businesses were noted on the map, including the Water Sports Company.

"Look, that's the actually name of the business, the *Water Sports Company*," said Murph.

"Well, that should be easy to find, but I don't see much around to hide us as we watch for Apollo," said Cap.

"There's a bar next to the place, but probably not a good choice for four Americans to go and have a drink," said Murph.

"We need something that won't stand out," Aliah added as she looked around.

"Hold on. An idea is coming to me," said Pyle.

She pointed to a delivery truck that was pulling into the market lot. They watched as the delivery boy, maybe nineteen years old, got out of the old truck and carried a box of vegetables into the market. The guys made their way to the truck and stood close, waiting for the boy to return. When he did, Cap spoke to him.

"Excuse me. Do you speak English?" Cap asked.

"Yes, I do," stated the boy.

"How would you like to make one hundred US dollars?" continued Cap.

"One hundred dollars," the boy repeated. "That is more than I make in two weeks delivering fruits and vegetables for my uncle."

Cap reached in his pocket and pulled out the money.

"What do I have to do?" asked the boy, eyeing the money.

"We need to rent your truck for a few hours," said Cap, dangling the bill in the air in front of the boy.

"My truck, I have two deliveries left, and if they are late, my uncle will make me pay for them," said the boy.

"How much?" asked Cap.

"Ten bucks, US," replied the boy.

"Okay, we will cover that too," said Cap, pulling another twenty out of his pocket.

The boy, catching on, replied, "Okay, I will take one hundred to rent the truck and twenty to cover my deliveries, but I will need one hundred more for me. In case I have to share with my uncle."

Cap realized the boy was sharp and didn't even argue. He coughed up the two hundred and twenty dollars and handed it to the young entrepreneur.

The boy flipped Cap the keys and started to walk away.

"Where do we leave the truck?" asked Cap.

"Just leave it here. I will come back in the morning to get it," said the boy as he continued to walk on down the street.

Although Cap stood in the parking lot, watching as the young man disappeared, the rest of the guys piled into the old truck that smelled of rotten fruit. Satisfied that the boy wasn't going to go and warn someone they were coming, Cap stepped into the truck's cab and turned the ignition. The truck came to life with a bang and a large puff of black smoke. Shifting the gears, he pressed on the gas, and the car started lumbering down the road past the port entrance. A few yards from the port entrance, he stopped on the street near the bar and across from the scuba place. Because he wasn't sure how quickly they would have to leave, he left the motor running. Periodically, the truck would belch gas and bang.

"Glad we got water at the market, but I sure hope no one has to go to the bathroom soon," said Pyle

"Well, thanks for bringing that up. Now I need to go," said Murph.

"I hope you can hold it because I see someone we know," said Cap, pointing to a man walking up to the scuba shop.

"That's friggin' Eurie from the bazaar," said Aliah.

"If that bastard runs his mouth," stopped Cap in mid-sentence.

Eurie entered the building, and the team waited. Murph no longer need to go to the bathroom. The adrenaline kicked in, and he was fine.

The team waiting as several people came in and out of the shop. But no Apollo or Eurie.

"I hate we can't see the back of the building, just these two sides," said Cap.

"We just need a little of your luck, Murph," said Aliah.

And almost on cue, Eurie walked out of the shop, but he was not alone. He was with Apollo and two other men. They walked a couple blocks away from the shop, only pausing enough he see what the loud bang behind them was.

"This damn truck is going to get us killed!" said Murph.

Apollo and his group, accustomed to the sounds of the delivery truck, just ignored it, turned, and continued to walk away from the shop. The delivery truck followed and finally pulled to the curb in front of a fish market.

"Looks like they are going into that building," said Pyle.

The building was a single-story structure with a single entrance on the front. From the one side, there were only windows and no doors.

"Murph, I know it's a risk, but I want to drive around the block to see the other two sides. You think you can step into this market and not get us blown?" asked Cap.

"No problem, just give me the map," said Murph.

Cap handed him the map, and he stepped out of the back of the delivery truck. Cap never shut off the engine and pulled out to circle the block. Murph stepped into the market with the map spread out in front of him. There was three people in the market, and they all stopped and looked at him when he entered. He went to the person closest to the door.

"Do you speak English?" he asked the clerk while keeping a peripheral watch on the building.

"Yes," replied the clerk.

"I am looking for a car rental place, and I don't see one on the map the cruise ship gave me," he stated.

The other two people in the store went about their business as the clerk tried to explain to Murph that the car rental place was near the airport and not the port. Murph played along, asking stupid questions until he saw the delivery truck coming back down the side street.

"Okay, thank you," he said abruptly and walked out the store.

Murph walked down a little and ran up behind the passing truck. Aliah opened the doors and helped him jump into the slow-moving truck.

"The other two sides are like these. Windows on the sides and entrances on opposite ends, but the entrance on the other side has a chain through the handles," reported Cap.

"So it can only be opened from the outside, leaving this door as the only way in or out. How you want to do it?" asked Murph.

"The building looks abandoned, but we have to be careful of innocent bystanders. The back-side entrance being locked leads me to believe they are the only people in there," replied Cap.

"But it also means that's the only way in for us without cutting that chain," he added.

"At least if that door is locked, it will keep the bad guys from slipping out once the party starts," added Murph.

"Get ready. I don't know what we will find in there. Hopefully, just Apollo, Eurie, and the other two men," said Cap.

"Let's stay silent as long as we can. Keep your eyes open, and remember, Apollo is our target. I don't know if our guys are in here, but they are our priority," he added.

The team pulled the truck near the building and opened the rear doors. They sprinted to the entrance and stacked up on the side of the double doors.

Cap motioned for Murph to open the door, and the rest entered. Murph fell into the stack at the end. Inside the doors, they found themselves in a large empty room with two doors. Murph eased up to the small window in one of the doors and reported back to the group.

"Looks like a long hallway with doors on both sides," he stated.

"Looks the same over here," reported Cap after looking through the other door's window.

"I want you two to go down this hallway, and Aliah and myself will go down the other," Cap said to Murph and Pyle.

"The hallway is dark, but there seems to be a room halfway down that has lights on," added Cap.

The team split into two and started down the adjacent hallways.

Murph and Pyle worked their way slowly down the hallway, checking doors as they passed. All were locked and appeared to be empty.

Cap and Aliah were doing the same procedure down their hallway. Periodically, they checked to see if any sounds were coming out of the locked rooms. They were working their way toward the lighted room.

Suddenly three men came out of the room and lit up the hallway. The brightness gave them enough warning to flatten themselves against opposing doorways. The three men approached the spot where the team stood pressed against the wall. There was no room to duck into and no time to turn and hide. Murph looked at Pyle and pulled his Ka-Bar from its sleeve. He placed his finger to his lips and motioned the universal quiet sign.

Cap and Aliah had the same issue, except there were only two men. Aliah was able to step into a doorway that was a little larger than the others. She pulled her knife, and they waited for the two men to get close. When they did, they saw Cap and went to pull their weapons. Aliah stepped out of the darkness and grabbed the closest man around his mouth and slid her knife into his throat. She forced the blade outward, cutting his vocal cords and ending his life. Cap reached out and grabbed the surprised man's hand that was still pulling his pistol. With one motion, he jammed his blade upward through the man's jaw and into his brain. Cap and Aliah rolled the two lifeless men close to the wall so they could partially hide the bodies from any observers down the hall.

It was a little tougher on the other side of the building. When the threesome got closer to Murph and Pyle, one man pulled his pistol. Pyle stepped out and slammed her rifle butt into his face, knocking him out. Murph grabbed the second and drove his blade through his side just below his armpit. He grabbed the man's mouth to keep him from calling out as he repeated the motion a few more times. The third man punched Pyle in the face, knocking her to the ground.

"Come here, you little bitch," he said to her as he kneeled over to grab her.

Pyle kicked the man in the knee, forcing it to the side with a sickening snap. Before he could even let out a scream, she spun on the ground, sweeping his feet out from underneath him and making him land facedown on the floor. Pyle rolled over on top of him and grabbed his gun strap that held his automatic rifle. She pulled the strap around his throat, creating a makeshift garrot. She pulled the strap like she was fighting to secure a runaway stagecoach from the old west movies she watched as a child.

Eventually, she a heard a snap, and the man's body went limp as his life passed.

"Who's the bitch now?" she said as she released her grasp on the strap.

Then a she heard a gunshot behind her.

She turned to see the first man she had knocked out slump to the ground. Murph stood there with his pistol smoking.

"No choice," he said, and they both started running toward the light.

Cap and Aliah had heard the single gunshot. One shot probably meant it was his guys and not the bad guys, but either way, whoever was in the lit room knew they were coming. They started running toward the room.

Murph and Pyle got there first. Murph took out a man that poked his head into the hallway. Cap and Aliah, who came running from the other side of the building, were in time to see Eurie standing there with a gun in his hand. He dropped it immediately when he saw Cap. Cap, however, wasn't paying attention to Eurie; he knew his teammates would handle him. What had Cap's attention was the large man who was standing between two of the six beds in the room. It was Apollo, and he held a bloody knife above one of the occupants. Without wasting a second, Cap aimed and fired his gun, hitting Apollo in the shoulder. Murph and Pyle entered and put Eurie on the ground. Apollo and Eurie were the only two men left in the room.

Cap walked over and dragged Apollo away from the beds.

"Set him up," Cap said to Murph about Eurie.

Murph pulled a metal chair to the center of the room and kicked Eurie on the side. "Get in the chair," he said.

Eurie responded and sat in the chair; he paused a moment to see if there was a sink anywhere around.

"And put this piece of shit in a chair too," said Cap as he dropped Apollo on the floor near Eurie.

Pyle and Aliah checked the occupants of the beds. McBeth, Reaper, and the other men were not there, but six young girls were. Each was tied in the beds by their hands over their heads. Apollo apparently had stabbed one girl and was working his way toward the next when Cap stopped him. The lifeless young girl just stared at the ceiling, never uttering a sound as her life had slipped away. The other five girls were still alive but seemed to be drugged. They slightly responded as Aliah and Pyle cut them free and sat them up in their beds one by one.

Murph and Cap had Apollo and Eurie secured in metal chairs.

"I need to know where my people are," said Cap to Apollo.

"I ain't saying shit to you," he responded.

"The only way you will make it out of here alive is to tell me," said Cap, poking his finger into the open wound on Apollo's shoulder.

Apollo refused to respond to the poke even though it had to have been painful and said," Do what you want. I have nothing to say to you."

Realizing Apollo wasn't going to cooperate, Cap turned to Eurie.

"Eurie, what do you know about where my people are?" said Cap.

Apollo just looked at Eurie. "You know these people?" he asked a nervous Eurie.

"No, I swear I do not know them," said Erie in a trembling voice.

Cap watched the exchange between the two. There might be a way to work Eurie's fear to get the information he needed.

"Okay, here's the deal. Whoever tells me where my people are will live. The other I shoot," said Cap, stepping back and pulling his pistol.

"You can shoot me if you want. He will never speak because he fears me," said Apollo.

"You don't get it. If he speaks, there is no more you to fear," answered Cap.

"Sir, I do not know where your friends are. Apollo never told me who he sold them to," said a crying Eurie.

Eurie knew that if Cap said one would live and one would die, he meant it.

"I told you he will not help you," responded Apollo, smiling.

"I don't know, but I do know where he keeps his records," said Eurie, which turned Apollo's smile into an immediate frown.

"You disloyal bastard. I will kill you for helping them," he said.

"Looks like I made a deal with Eurie, and you lose, Apollo," said Cap as he pointed the pistol to Apollo's head.

"Wait," said Apollo, seeing his plight. "If I give you a name, will that work?"

"A name," said Cap.

"Yes, the name of the man that bought your friends," responded Apollo.

"Well, it won't hurt your situation. That's for sure," responded Cap.

"The deal was, I give you information, and I live. This bastard will die," stated Apollo.

"That is the deal," answered Cap. "So give me the name, and that completes our deal," he added.

"Ntaganda, Sani Ntaganda," said Apollo.

"Isn't that the warlord from Mali?" asked Murph.

"That is him," said Apollo. "He contacted my people and said he wanted some US soldiers to publicly execute. When we found out the people trying to rescue these girls were soldiers, we knew we had a chance to score some big bucks. It's all about the money in my business," he continued.

Disgusted with what he was observing, Murph moved forward. "We should have ended that dude when we had the chance," said Murph.

"The warlord has our friends. Is he taking them back to Mali?" asked Cap.

"I don't know. I know he was still in Mali when Yassin contacted him," said Apollo.

"Yassin. What the hell is he doing in all this?" blasted Cap.

"He showed up and wanted to buy the soldiers himself, but I had already made a deal with Ntaganda. He called Ntaganda to try and buy them, but he wouldn't sell them. Especially when Yassin told him that two of the men I had were the soldiers that had been in his camp before. I think he wants revenge," he added.

"But Yassin doesn't have any of my friends," asked Cap, once again poking the injury.

"No," cried Apollo

"Cap, we got what we need. We know they are in Mali. We need to get these girls out of here," said Murph.

"Can they walk?" Cap asked Aliah.

"Yes, but not too fast," she replied.

"Okay, let's move them out to the delivery truck," said Cap. "I hope Arthur's driver doesn't mind a couple extra passengers."

Aliah and Pyle got the five girls to their unsteady feet and started walking them out.

"Girls, we are taking you out of here. Please follow the nice ladies out to our truck, and we will get you all home," said Cap to the scared girls.

"I think it's beginning to sink in what's going on," said Pyle

"Murph, you lead them out, and Pyle and Aliah will help the girls. I'm staying a minute to deal with Apollo and Eurie," said Cap.

Murph paused for a minute and just looked at Cap before he led the group out of the room.

"Now you will set me free and shoot this bastard," said Apollo to Cap.

"I did make a deal that I would shoot the one that didn't talk and not the other one," said Cap as he raised his pistol and shot Eurie in the meaty part of his shoulder.

"Don't worry, Eurie. It's just a flesh wound, and you will live," said Cap.

"Oh, no, he won't. When I get free from this chair, I am going to break your neck," said Apollo to Eurie.

Cap cut Eurie's bonds and said, "Go, but if we ever cross paths again, you will not be so lucky."

"I will find you!" yelled Apollo as Eurie ran out of the room, holding his shoulder.

"Now cut me lose," said Apollo. "We had a deal," he added.

"We did have a deal. I stuck to it. I said the first to talk, I shoot the other one. I shot Eurie," said Cap.

"You can't leave me tied up like this. When I get free, I will make sure you never find your friends," said Apollo.

"I know," said Cap as he pointed his pistol at Apollo and shot him mid forehead. Cap didn't wait to watch the life bleed out of Apollo because he knew if he had let Apollo live, the large man would constantly be getting in their way. Getting rid of trash was always better done sooner than later.

Cap got to the truck just as the last girl was loaded.

"What happened?" asked Murph

"Just tying up loose ends. Let's get out of here," said Cap.

Murph drove the delivery truck back to the waiting tour bus. The group filed out of the truck and got on the bus.

"A few extra passengers. Are these the people you came for?" asked the driver.

The group settled in for the drive back to Bucharest.

Cap looked over at Aliah, who still had blood on her hands from the hallway. Aliah was trying to wipe it off on her pant leg.

"First time up close and personal?" asked Cap.

"Yes" was all she said.

"I won't say it gets easier because it doesn't, but it should make it easier knowing what hell those men put these girls through and the hundreds before them," said Cap.

Aliah just nodded and went back to looking after the girls.

"Cap, you need to come over here," said Pyle.

"This young lady's name is Elizabeth Anderson," announced Pyle.

"Hello, Elizabeth. We are fiends of your aunt," said Cap. "She's told us all so much about you," he added, taking her hand.

"Are you the man she calls Mr. Rogers?" asked Elizabeth.

"My last name is Rodgers. I've been a friend of your aunt for a few years," he replied.

"Mister Rogers, boy, I can only image the conversation McBeth and her sister have had about you," said Murph with a little chuckle.

"Are you taking us home now?" said Elizabeth.

Her frail body looked dwarfed by the seat in which she sat. It was obvious that she and many of the girls hadn't been fed well. *Stupid*, Cap thought. The men who had captured these girls evidently weren't good businessman since they had damaged the merchandise. Cap couldn't help but wonder what had caused Apollo to knife the one girl. It was a question that would have to wait, and a question that probably would never be answered now that Apollo was dead.

Redirecting his attention to Elizabeth, he answered her question. "Yes, we have a plane waiting that will get you to a safe place and back to your mom."

Elizabeth laid down in her seat and closed her eyes. The girls had obviously been given something at the house to keep them compliant.

From the front of the bus, the driver turned to address Cap. "I called Arthur and told him we were headed back. He said not to come back to the office but meet him at a different spot. The word is already out that Apollo and several of his men are dead. His people are looking for you."

"I need to speak to the countess," said Cap.

"No need. She will be waiting with the limo and has everything under control, as she put it," responded the driver.

Cap shook his head and thought, *Gotta love that woman.*

Turning back to the wheel, the driver maneuvered the bus through the narrow streets and headed toward the rendezvous point. The passengers on the bus remained silent; some were thinking about McBeth, Reaper, and their missing friends. Some were thinking about the poor girls they had rescued. However, it wasn't too long before the bus met up with where the countess waited. When they arrived, they saw the limo with Arthur and the countess standing beside it.

The bus pulled up, and Cap was the first off.

"You guys sure have stirred up things around here," said Arthur.

"Did you find your people?" asked the countess.

"No, but we know where they are headed. We did find the little girl that our people were after," said Cap as the group filed off the bus.

"Five extra passengers going to be a problem?" Cap asked the countess. "They are in pretty bad shape. Whatever drug Apollo gave them is still in their systems, and they appear to be quite malnourished. Those idiots weren't feeding the girls regularly, and I bet the girls have been exposed to a lot of other mistreatments as well. They are going to need medical and psychiatric treatment."

"No problem for the plane. It's big enough, but maybe getting them onboard is going to be difficult," she replied.

"Even if it's a diplomatic flight?" asked Cap.

"Yes, they only allow the people that came in on the flight to leave on it," she stated.

"We need to get them home," said Cap.

"Load them up in the limo. I will make this happen," said the confident countess.

They all got into the limo with Arthur driving. It took a few minutes to get to the airport since they had to work their way as to avoid any check points. Eventually, the limo rolled up to the gate, and Arthur announced the countess was returning to her plane. The gate opened, and the limo proceeded to her plane. At the plane, there were four airport security guards standing perimeter of her plane.

"Pull the limo close to the stairs to the plane, and everyone stay quiet and stay in the limo until I signal you," said the countess.

She exited the limo and saw the guard from the arrival.

"Hello, my dear friend. How are you?" she asked, walking up to him with her outreached hand.

The guard was taken back by her kindness and said, "I am very well. How are you?"

"I am fantastic. What a great trip I have had in your beautiful country." She fanned herself and leaned forward as if she were going to share some confidence with the guard. Almost like a reflex reaction, he too leaned forward. "And I thank you and your men for watching over my plane," the countess added. "If you ever want to visit my country, I would love to show you the beauty of my home. I live on a nice estate that would make a great vacation spot for you and your families."

She signaled to the other guards, who looked like they were eager to hear what the countess was saying. She had deliberately lowered her voice to create a sense of intimacy. Within seconds, she had all the guards close to her and was inviting them all to bring their families to vacation at her home.

"I want you all to know how much I appreciate your kindnesses."

"You are very welcome, Countess. Is your group ready to leave?" the first guard asked, looking at the limo, a little surprised her security team was not out with her.

"I am. My people are talking on the phone, making flight arrangements, and I told them I wished to speak to you alone. They have been with me long enough that they know when I say I want to be alone with someone that I mean they are to stay back. Of course, if you weren't respected guards, they wouldn't have left me alone. Arthur, you know him, I bet. He works for one of your country's biggest charities. He told them I was safe with you," she stated.

"Anyway, I would like to take a picture of you to display in my office. Would it be possible to get a picture of me and your team? I keep a book of photos of special people I meet when I travel," she continued.

Flattered by the invitation and impressed by the countess's desire for their photo, the guards complied with the countesses wishes.

Once the guards had gathered, the countess signaled for Arthur to come take the picture. She placed Arthur several feet away from the limo and purposely had him stand facing the limo, so when she and the guards posed, they would be looking in the opposite direction. When Arthur raised his hand to get the guards and the countess' attention to smile for the photo, Murph and Aliah took the first two girls up the stairs and into the plane. Seeing that they needed more time, Arthur said the photo was blurry, and he needed another. When he raised his hand again, Pyle took the next two girls into the plane. That left Cap and Elizabeth in the limo.

The countess again thanked the guards. She gave each one of them one of her calling cards. "When you want to come, just contact the person on this card, and she will make the arrangements."

The guards once more thanked the countess then began walking back to resume their positions. Before they had gotten far, Cap stepped out of the limo. The look on his face let the countess know he need a little more time, so she stopped and said to Arthur.

"I really would like you in the picture. Excuse me," she said to Cap standing by the limo. "Would you mind taking a picture of us?" she coyly asked.

Cap, seeing where she was going with that, responded, "Yes, Countess," and he called for Murph to come out of the plane and get the last piece of luggage for the countess.

Cap walked over, and the countess arranged everyone for the final picture.

"Whenever you are ready," she said.

Murph got ready to make his move, and Cap raised his hand to get their attention.

"Everyone, look at the camera and say cheese," he said.

The group responded, and Murph snatched Elizabeth out of the limo and climbed into the plane faster than Cap could take the picture.

The countess thanked everyone, kissed Arthur farewell, and went into her plane, waving at the men still standing in a group.

Cap entered the pane and closed the door behind him.

"That was smooth," said Murph to the countess.

She just curtsied and took a seat.

"That is one spectacular individual," said Murph to Cap.

"Yes, she is," said Cap. "Let's get these ladies home," he added, and the plane took off, leaving Romania.

CHAPTER 7

NORTH KOREA

McBeth tried to focus, but she was too drugged. Her last clear memory was the injection gun being jammed into her neck, and the rest became cloudy. She slightly remembered things like being dragged across the floor and placed in a box. She remembered the jostling and gentle swaying that had rocked her back to sleep. She remembered hearing the faint cries of what seemed to be little girls calling out to anyone who would listen. Then she would fall asleep and wake to silence, not a regular silence but the kind that was created to keep you from hearing anything.

As she was coming out from under the control of the drug, she realized she was in a wooden box, and the box must have been loaded into a container. She had no concept of time. It could have been hours or days since she started her journey. Then the moving stopped. A bright light shone through her breathing holes, and she felt the box she was in being unloaded from the container and carried. Through the holes, she could see there was several men all dressed in black, hustling around, unloading several other containers. Some had wooden boxes, and some carried cardboard boxes; there was no clue of their contents. Her box hit the truck bed hard, and it bounced her head off the top of the box. She moved closer to the hole to get a wider view of the operation. Another box sat down next to her, and all she could see was a bright-blue, tear-filled eye looking back at hers.

"Are you okay?" she asked the blue eye.

A little voice said, "I think so, but I want to go home."

"Me too, sweetheart, but we have to stay strong. My name is McBeth. What's yours?" she asked.

"My name is Amelia," said the little girl.

"Where are you from, Amelia?" asked McBeth.

"London. My family is in London. They are going to be so mad at me for wandering off," said the frantic little girl.

"No, they won't, Amelia. They will be so glad to get you home, and I promise we will get out of here," responded McBeth, trying to calm Amelia.

"No talking," said one of the armed men as he slammed his rifle butt down on Amelia's wooden prison. The noise caused her to scream and start crying again.

The truck started moving, and between the noise and the bumping around, there was no more talking. It seemed to be hours the truck sped along the back roads until finally it rolled onto a paved road. It was only a few minutes, and the truck stopped and started backing toward a building. The truck stopped short of the building and men started climbing onto the back of the truck. One by one, the wooden boxes were opened and the occupants taken inside. McBeth was dragged into the building with her hands and feet still tied. Still somewhat under the effects of the drug, she had no opportunity to attempt an escape. She was taken into a room with six beds and placed in metal chair in the center of the room. Her hands and feet where retied to the chair, and she couldn't move. McBeth recognized Amelia from her amazingly blue eyes. She was already in the room and sitting on a bed with her hands tied to the headboard.

She looked at McBeth and whimpered, "Are you McBeth?"

"Yes, Amelia, I am," responded McBeth. It seemed to calm Amelia down just seeing her.

The men brought one more girl into the room and placed her on the empty bunks. There were two girls already there.

"One of you girls need to explain the rules to the new ones," said one of the armed men. He walked over and patted one of the original girls on the head and said, "I'm sure I will see you later," and walked out.

The other girl spoke up, "We have to follow all the orders without question. If anyone yells, screams, or cried loudly, the guards will come in here."

"Do they beat you?" asked one of the other new girls.

"No, they want to keep us ready to move, so they won't beat us. They will beat her and do much worse," said the girl, pointing to the other girl tied to the bunk.

"Why do they beat her?" questioned McBeth.

"Raise your head, Cindy," said the girl who had been explaining the rules.

The girl named Cindy raised her head and displayed a large cut across her cheek.

"She's unsellable, so they use her to punish us if we don't do what they say," said the girl.

"It happens every day they find a reason to punish us. They make us watch as they beat or torture Cindy," said the girl.

Cindy never spoke a word. She just lowered her head and sat quietly on her bunk.

"Damn animals," said McBeth.

"They will be here in a few hours, and we will have to change into our party dresses. Then they will take us to potential buyers. It happens every night. Sometimes girls come back, and sometimes they are gone," continued the girl.

"That's crazy," said McBeth.

"Please don't argue with them. They will simply leave you tied and make you watch them abuse Cindy. Sometimes it two or three guards at a time. And if you say anything, they beat her more," said the girl.

The room stayed quiet for a long time. Then the guards came. They laid out dresses for the five girls. Not one for Cindy or McBeth.

"No party for you," said one of the men, stroking McBeth's hair. "We have bigger plans for you," he added.

Amelia couldn't hold it back anymore and started crying. Cindy immediately started saying, "No, no, no."

The closest guard looked at Amelia and said, "This is what happens when you don't follow instructions."

He stepped over to Cindy and grabbed her by her hair and forced her back on the bed. She went totally limp in anticipation to what was about to happen. The guard then called for another guard to join him. A third guard entered and stood by, watching the other girls. As the two started having their way with the lifeless Cindy, McBeth tried to look away, knowing if she spoke up, it would be worse for Cindy. Amelia started to cry harder.

"You have to stop," yelled the girl to Amelia. "The more you cry, the worse they will treat her. That's how they control us," she added.

McBeth looked at Amelia and said, "You have to calm down, please."

"I'm trying," she said as the terrible events unfolded in front of her.

The guards finished, and the main offender said to the girls, "Anyone else have anything to say? I'm sure Cindy can take another round or two."

All the girls and McBeth nodded in compliance.

"Good. Take showers and put on the dresses. While you're at it, clean her up too. I want her fresh for round two tonight," said the guard.

McBeth thought, *What kind of hell have these girls lived in?* She didn't think they could handle much more. She hoped help was on its way.

CHAPTER 8

ROAD TO AUSTRIA

Callie ran into Smitty's office, carrying the sat phone. "It's Cap." She was out of breath after running up two flights of stairs. She handed him the phone.

"Hey, brother, what's the good news?" asked Smitty.

"The good news is, we found McBeth's niece, and she's on the plane with us, headed back to Austria," said Cap.

"Bad news is, we didn't find our people. Looks like they sold them to Ntaganda in Africa," he continued.

"Ntaganda, the warlord?" asked Smitty.

"Yes, it looks like he was in the market for some US soldiers for some revenge," said Cap.

"Jesus, we better get a move on before the madman does something to them," stated Smitty.

"How fast can you get the guys on the big plane?" asked Cap.

"We can be ready within the hour. I've had them all standing by here, waiting," added Smitty.

"Can you get with Rebolini and update him?" asked Cap.

"He's right here. We've all been waiting to hear from you," said Smitty.

"Great. We will see you in Austria in a few hours. I was thinking, since Apollo told me they smuggled them into Africa crossing the Black Sea, maybe we need to call an expert and pick his brain about the best routes for us to take," suggested Cap.

"Good idea. I'm pretty sure Rebolini has Amir's new number," replied Smitty.

72

Smitty hung up the sat phone and turned to Rebolini.

"They have the girl, but no luck with the team. Cap says the Apollo dude sold them to the warlord in Mali for some revenge propaganda bullshit. I don't like it. If he has them, they could already be dead. He wants us to meet him in Austria and plan the rescue," said Smitty.

"What was the part about Amir?" asked Rebolini.

"Cap suggested we contact Amir to pick his brain about the routes into Mali," replied Smitty.

"Okay, I'll call Amir and get the teams rolling. Do you think this Apollo guy is telling the truth?" said Rebolini.

"Cap is counting on it," said Smitty as he left the room to gather the team.

Rebolini went to his desk and looked up Amir's number. He dialed and waiting for an answer.

The phone only rang a few times before someone answered it.

"Hello, is this Amir Zahira?" asked Rebolini.

"Who is asking?" said a deep voice.

"This is Colonel Rebolini from the Divine Group," stated Rebolini.

"Oh. Hello, Colonel. This is Amir," said Amir.

"I hope you and your families are doing fine. I need to ask you for a favor," asked Rebolini.

"Anything," said Amir.

"Cap and the guys need some information about the predominate routes you use getting into Mali with goods," asked Rebolini.

"From which direction is he entering?" asked Amir.

"It looks like he's planning to enter through the Black Sea area," answered Rebolini.

"There are so many little rivers that run off the Black Sea. If you give me an email, I can send you a map with the routes highlighted," responded Amir.

"I will give you Cap's email. He is in Austria, waiting for the team to join him. I know you remember McBeth and Reaper," said Rebolini, pausing for a minute.

"Yes, I remember them well," said Amir.

"It looks like our old friend, the warlord, has them hostage and is planning some type of revenge," continued Rebolini.

"Revenge! You mean he plans to kill them because they rescued my family?" asked Amir.

"It's not your fault they are in trouble, but we do need to try and save them," said Rebolini.

"I have to help. I can't just sit here in my new home in Turkey and let them die because they helped me," said Amir.

"Amir, it's not your fault, but we do need information about the smuggling routes in that area. I'll text you Cap's email, and thank you," said Rebolini.

"I will have the info to you in less than an hour. I will mark the routes on a map and email you as soon as I finish. I am in your team's debt, so you are more than welcome, my friend, and may God bless you and the guys," replied Amir.

Rebolini hung up the phone and texted the email address to Amir's phone. Amir responded that he received the email.

Rebolini made one more phone call.

"Good morning, Colonel," said the female voice on the phone.

"Good morning, Madam President. I have a little update on the Romania thing if you have time," said Rebolini. Before Rebolini had left the White House, President Campbell had given him her private phone number with an admonition to keep it private.

"I can make the time," replied the president.

"The guys located the missing girl, but not the team. We were right. It wasn't the Romanian government. It was a smuggling syndicate. Cap was able to find out that the smugglers sold the team to an African warlord named Ntaganda for some revenge show he plans to put on. They are assembling in Austria to plan a rescue attempt into Mali," said Rebolini.

"Mali is a hot spot for trouble. I wish them the best, but you know we can't officially back your guys. I hate it, but it's the international politic game we have to play to keep the UN off our back," replied the president.

"Ma'am, with all due respect, I don't believe the UN, US, or that warlord could keep these guys from going into Mali," said Rebolini.

"Tell them good luck and Godspeed," said the president.

"Will do, ma'am," replied Rebolini.

Rebolini hung up from the president and went to join Smitty and the team. They were loading their gear into the truck to head to the airport.

"I talked to Amir, and he is sending Cap a map of the routes. I will be standing by in our command center for any assistance you guys will need. I checked in with the Lady, and she wished you and the team luck. Remember, I can still get some unofficial help, but if you run into trouble, you are on your own," continued Rebolini.

The guys started getting on the truck, and Rebolini stopped the new guy.

"We haven't had a chance to meet in person, but I'm Marcus Rebolini," he said to Cooper. Cooper was a tall man with dark, penetrating eyes. He wore army fatigues that hugged his muscled frame.

"Hello, sir, I'm Mark Cooper. It's a pleasure to meet you," said Cooper.

"Nice to meet you, Cooper. Welcome to our team," replied Rebolini.

"Thank you, sir, but please call me Coop," stated Coop as he shook Rebolini's hand and jumped into the back of the truck.

"Let me know if you need anything and see you when you get back," said Rebolini as he waved at the team leaving.

Twenty minutes later, the truck pulled up to the *big plane* as Cap called it. The plane was kept in the general aviation part of the airport. That allowed the team access to drive a vehicle right up to the doors to load. It also allowed them to take gear on the plane that normally wouldn't be allowed in an airport. Michelena and Callie were the pilots for this flight and had already prepped the plane and filed their flight plan to Austria.

"Let's get the gear stowed away ASAP. The faster we get loaded, the faster we get airborne. It's a long flight to Austria. Hope you brought something to read or listen to," said Smitty. "I suggest you take advantage of the opportunity to rest because once we get there, who knows when you will get to relax again."

The team settled in for the flight. Michelena taxied the plane down the runway and waited for tower approval to takeoff. Once they gave the go-ahead, the plane was in the air in seconds.

Meanwhile, in the air, headed to Austria from the other side of the world, Cap spoke to the group.

"Smitty has the rest of the team headed this way. The plan is to land in Austria and get these girls out of the country as quickly as possible to England. We have people standing by in the US Embassy there to get them home," said Cap.

"If you need these poor young girls taken to England, why didn't you just ask? It would be my pleasure to take them home," stated the countess.

"You never fail to amaze me," said Cap to the countess, kissing her on the cheek.

"When we get to Austria, Murph and I will stand by for the team to arrive. Pyle, I want you and Aliah to escort these girls home," said Cap.

"Yes, sir," said Pyle and Aliah.

"I can have my driver take you to my house so you can rest until your team gets here," said the countess.

"That would be fantastic, and thank you," said Murph. "These guys need a hot shower," he added, thumbing his nose at Cap in jest.

The pilot called back and said they were starting their descent into the airport. They would be on the ground in fifteen minutes.

The countess picked up her direct phone to the pilot and said, "We will be refueling and heading right back out to London, England. Please complete the flight plan."

She hung up the phone and looked at the tired and weary young girls. "Anything special you want me to get you while we are refueling to head home?" she asked the girls.

It seemed pizza and soda were the favorite choice. So the countess put in a request with the pilots.

Finally, the wheels touched down with a screech, and the plane taxied to the private terminal. Murph and Cap were met by the countess' limo, and the girls had a chance to step out of the plane into the private hanger for their first breath of freedom. They laughed a little and hugged each other. They didn't let go until they saw the table full of pizzas and soda.

Cap and Murph left the girls laughing and getting drunk off their first taste of caffeine in a while.

"I hate to be on that plane with eight caffeinated women," said Murph.

Cap just laughed. "I am just glad the girls can still laugh. God help them. You know it is going to be rough for them to readjust to freedom. They will be haunted for nightmares for the rest of their lives." He looked over at the girls and found himself smiling because they were feasting on the pizza and giggling.

Once the plane was refueled, the girls got back onboard, and the plane took off for London.

Cap and Murph headed away from the airport, both quiet as they planned and schemed the best way to rescue their friends. Once they arrived at the countess' home, they were immediately met by her servants at the front door. Without delay, the two were shown their separate rooms. Each room had its own master bath complete with Jacuzzi. Murph showered quickly and requested something to eat. They brought the food to his room like room service at a five-star hotel. He ate and went to sleep.

Cap also ordered food after his long shower, but there was no sleep in his future. For the first time, he sat and allowed his worries about McBeth to surface. He was mad and scared at the same time. Mad because she didn't confide in him about her plans and scared he would never see her again. He tried to push those thoughts out of his head, but he knew it wasn't happening. He tried to pass the time watching TV but couldn't understand what they were saying, so he turned that off. All the people he spent his time with were in flight or lost. He sat in a chair, just looking out a tall window that revealed the green lawn that spread across the panorama. Eventually, his body forced him to fall asleep, and he slept for several hours until his sat phone rang and startled him. Still sitting in the chair, he answered.

"Cap, we are forty-five minutes away," said Smitty

"Great. We will meet you at the airport. Tell the pilot to taxi to hangar 36. That's the countess' private terminal," said Cap as he struggled to get out of the chair.

He got dressed and banged on Murph's door. "Let's roll. The team will be here in thirty minutes," he said as he went down the hallway to the main entrance.

"We need a ride back to the airport," he told one of the servants.

"A car has been on standby per the countess' request," said the servant. For a few seconds, Cap thought about how all the countess' servants he had met spoke English, then he let the thought go. *More important things to think about*, he told himself.

Soon Murph joined Cap at the door, and they both jumped into the limo.

"I received an email from Amir. Rebolini asked him to send us the smuggling routes into Mali. His email was very vague but stated he had someone that would meet us here," Cap pointed the place out on the map. "Once we get there, this guy will get us into Mali with no problem."

"I sure hope we are in time and that lunatic hasn't harmed the guys," said Murph.

Cap just shook his head, hoping the same thing. They didn't speak again until the airport.

Standing in front of the hangar, Murphy asked, "Are they bringing the big plane?"

"Look and see for yourself," said Cap as he pointed to the pink C-130 coming down the runway.

"I love that plane," said Murph.

"No, you love the pilots." Cap laughed as he smacked Murph on the back as the plane slowly rolled up to the hanger.

The plane came to a stop, and the rear doors opened. The team walked out and greeted Cap and Murph.

"Hey, guys," said Cap. "Welcome to Austria," he added.

They all shook hands and hugged.

"Let's step into the hanger and talk about our plan," said Cap, walking toward the hanger.

"I see the countess has a nice setup here," said Smitty. "Where is she?"

"She flew the girls to London on her private plane. Aliah and Pyle went to escort them to the US Embassy there," said Cap.

"That was very nice of her," stated Smitty.

"Buddy, you don't know the half of it. I will fill you in after we all get back home," said Cap.

The team all grabbed seats around a large wooden table.

"Guys, if you haven't met Coop, he the newest addition to the team," said Smitty, pointing out Coop sitting in the back.

"Welcome. We are putting you straight into the action on this one," Cap said.

"Wouldn't have it any other way, and I'm glad to be part of the team," responded Coop.

"Okay, back to business. We found out that the smugglers sold the guys to this warlord in Mali we dealt with a while back. He is looking to make some example out of the guys. We need to get there as soon as possible. We've contacted the doctor that was smuggling goods for the warlord. He's helping us get into Mali undetected," reported Cap.

"Our first step is to get to Mauritania. There we will be met by the doctor's guy to get us into Mali. There are so many routes, and the options change daily according to the doc," added Cap.

"How long before we take off?" asked Snyder.

"As soon as Michelena get the plane fueled, we leave," he answered.

"So hit the bathrooms, stretch your legs, do whatever you need because we are not waiting any longer than needed," said Smitty.

Within an hour, the big pink plane rolled down the runway and took off, heading to Mauritania.

"We have a two-hour flight and won't be on the ground very long. So get your gear ready for a fast deploy once we land. Amir's guy will have a truck waiting for us," said Cap over the roar of the engines.

The plane flew its course, and the team went about preparing their gear. There was not much talking since everyone was focusing on the task at hand.

After what seemed a short time, Callie spoke over the intercom, "We are starting our descent. It's a small-ass strip, and I bet it's bumpy. Better strap in tight."

"I sure hope there aren't any cows on the runway. Looking at a map, this is nothing but farmland with an old airstrip in the middle," said Callie to Michelena.

"I don't see any landing lights. Is this one that we click the mic, and the lights come on?" asked Callie.

"I don't think this place even has electricity," replied Michelena.

As the plane got lower, a series of lights started to illuminate.

"Someone is lighting the way," said Michelena.

"Get ready to land," Callie announced to the team.

They all tightened their seat straps and their grip on their weapons.

The plane touched down at the first light that resulted from a burning fifty-five-gallon barrel. The wind from the plane extinguished the fire as it passed. The plane bounced down the dirt runway, and Michelena and Callie stood on the brakes to stop it on the short runway. The plane came to a halt right at the end of the dirt, and slowly they turned the plane around in the wide spot on the end.

"That was fun," said Callie as Michelena just rolled her eyes.

Headlights from a truck appeared, heading to the plane.

"Guys, we got company," said Callie.

Cap, Murph, Coop, and Bain slid out the side door to make sure the visitor was friendly. The truck stopped in front of the plane, and the driver got out.

"Hello, my friends," said the driver.

"Amir, is that you?" asked Cap.

"Yes. Great to see you again," he said.

"I thought you were sending a guy to meet us," replied Cap.

"I couldn't trust anyone with this important task. It had to be me, and I owe you guys so much," responded Amir. "And besides, no one knows these routes like me. I'm the one who made them."

Cap returned to the plane, and Smitty went over to hug Amir.

"Okay, guys, let's unload our gear and get this plane out of here," ordered Cap.

The team loaded their equipment into the back of Amir's truck.

"We have about an hour's drive, then we will meet up with my contact. He and his friends will help us," said Amir.

"Are these people we can trust? asked Cap. "I know loyalty changes with the wind here, no disrespect to your friends," he added.

"These men hate the warlord and will do anything to get him out of the picture," continued Amir. "The one thing they despise is human trafficking, and that is one of the Ntaganda's most lucrative endeavors."

The team loaded up and started on their trek. The old truck bumped down the narrow dirt roads. It seemed the further it went, the narrower the roads. Eventually, the road turned to just two small strips of dirt and grass. Then it just became grass. The truck pulled into the tree line and stopped with just enough tree canopy to hide it from anyone looking. The team unloaded and gathered on Cap.

"When are your people getting here?" he asked Amir.

"We are a little early, but they should be here within the next thirty minutes," answered Amir.

"Everyone, double-check your gear. We have a few minutes before we move out," said Cap. Night was beginning to wane, and light was only a few hours away.

Amir came over to Cap and Smitty. He had an AK-47 slung over his shoulder.

"You know how to use that?" asked Smitty.

"Yes, you pull this, and the bullet come out there," answered Amir with a smile. "Seriously, I was required to serve five years in the Israeli Army before I could become a doctor. I am fully qualified to carry and use this weapon," said Amir, tapping his rifle.

"We hope you don't ever have to, but I want you to be prepared, just in case," said Cap.

A distant voice called out from the trees, and the team snapped into the alert mode. Rifles pointed, and everyone ducked for cover. All but Amir. He looked around and laughed then called out to the voice. A few seconds later, four men appeared from the foliage.

Amir walked up to the men and spoke to them. They then hugged and turned to walk back to the rest of the team.

"Cap, these are my friends," announced Amir.

Cap was just getting back on his feet. He reached out his hand to the men. They all shook, and Cap said, "Thank you all for helping us. Amir has said we have a common enemy."

The one man just spat and said, "We will do anything to get rid of that bastard."

"We need to get moving if we want to make our connections and meet up with the other men," said Amir.

"Other men?" questioned Smitty.

"Yes, when they found out we were going to the warlord's camp, several men wanted to come with us. All the men that are going have had a run-in with the warlord in the past," added Amir.

Cap turned to the team and said, "Let's get going. Amir and his men will take the lead. MK, you and Snyder take the rear," ordered Cap.

The group headed through the dense foliage with Amir leading. They traveled for an hour before stopping.

"We need to wait here until we get the signal the river is clear," said Amir to the team.

"We have a few minutes. Everyone, take a break," ordered Cap to the rest of the team.

"How far are we away from the river?" asked Cap.

"The river is very close. We have to make sure the African Army doesn't have a patrol near us," replied Amir.

A few minutes later, two of the men reappeared from the trees and spoke to Amir. Amir then went to Cap and Smitty.

"We have a small window, but we must go now," reported Amir.

Cap motioned for the team to move. The team followed Amir's friends through the trees. They moved fast so they wouldn't lose sight of men in front of them. Suddenly they came out of the tree line and were at the river. However, there were two fishing boats with armed men waiting on them.

"No one move," said the armed man on the first boat.

The team, taken by surprise, didn't have time to raise their weapons.

Cap thought to himself, *Here we go again. Is anyone trustworthy in the damn country!*

The men unloaded from the boats but kept their weapons pointed at the interlopers. Amir's friends, who led them through the trees into the ambush, were in just as much a pickle as the team was, but where was Amir?

The leader of the armed men shouted at the team, "Drop your weapons and put your hands on your head."

Amir's men complied immediately, but Cap's team was reluctant at first. One of the men came over and poked his rifle butt into Smitty's chest and demanded He drop his rifle. Smitty reacted as any Navy SEAL would when told to drop his rifle on the ground. He struck the man across the nose, which exploded like a fourth of July firecracker. The leader of the armed men turned to point his rifle at Smitty, but a whooshing sound came past Cap's head, and a knife suddenly struck the man in the back of the head. His dead finger clinched down on the trigger of his AK-47 and started shooting rounds wildly in the air and on the ground. One of Amir's guys was hit in the leg, and another man was struck in the back. In the chaos, Amir appeared from the foliage and cut the throat of the closest bad guy. He then fired two shots, striking two more of the armed assailants. Cap fired at the two men in the boat, and Smitty finished off the last man standing.

After the smoke cleared, Amir stood in the middle of what was the armed men's advantage point with a pistol in one hand and a bloody blade in the other.

Amir looked up at Cap and said, "Looked like you guys needed a little help."

Cap and Smitty look at each other. "I guess we can take worrying about you off our minds," said Smitty.

"Beginner's luck," replied Amir with a smile as he re-holstered his weapons.

Amir stepped over to bad guy that was hit in the back. "This one is still breathing," he said.

Cap joined him just as Amir was rolling him over.

"Why were you guys after us, and what does the warlord know about our plans?" asked Cap.

"We aren't with the warlord. We saw your guys in the trees and planned to rob you," said the squirming man. "I need a doctor," he continued.

"You are in luck. I'm a doctor," said Amir, which caused the man's eye to rise.

"You are a doctor?" repeated the man.

Amir leaned forward to examine the man's wound. Although light was now a pink strip crossing the sky, Amir leaned in close so he could examine the wound more clearly. "Yes, I am a doctor, and your injuries are not life-threatening—that is, if you get treated soon," continued Amir. He straightened back up and looked at the man lying on the ground.

"Tell us about your boats and where you came from," demanded Amir.

The wounded man told Amir that he and his buddies came from a small village down the stream from where they were now. He told Amir how he and his buddies stole from whomever they could. The warlord let them be if they paid him a part of what they stole.

"Looks like our secret is still safe. If you believe this man," said Cap to the team.

"He's afraid he's going to die, so I believe he is telling the truth," said Amir.

"As soon as we let him go, everyone will know we are here," said Smitty.

"True. We will have to either kill him or take him with us," said Amir, sliding his blade out of its sleeve.

"Not so fast, killer," said Cap.

"Let's put him in one of the boats with us, and if he becomes a problem, well, we will deal with him them," Cap added. "We will take their boats. Ours would stand out, and these are up and down this river all the time," he continued.

"We need to get a move on if we plan to make it there before the sunset," said Smitty.

The light from the rising sun continued to climb higher into the sky, sending shafts of light through the tall foliage surrounding the man. Some of it sparkled upon the waters, creating a surreal background for the men festooned with weapons, sweat, and blood.

Once Amir finished his bandage on the wounded man, he was loaded onto one of the boats. Amir's wounded friend was attended to but was too bad to make the trip. Instead, one of his buddies lifted the wounded man and carried him away while Cap and the others loaded onto the two boats headed north on the Niger toward the warlord's stronghold.

CHAPTER 9

WARLORD OF MALI

There is nothing like being wakened with cold water, Reaper thought as he spat up the water that was thrown on him. The foul odor assaulted his nostrils and sickened his stomach. He tried to take a deep breath to calm his stomach, but instead, the motion made him sicker. He leaned over toward his side and began to throw up. Since there wasn't much on his stomach, he convulsed as dry heaves racked his frame. He tried to sit up, thinking that might stop the heaving; but instead, the moment he moved his leg, another wave of nausea coursed through him. Finally, after minutes of dry heaves, his stomach calmed, and he was able to remain in an upright position. He wasn't sure how long he had been out, but while he had slept, his wounded leg had started bleeding and was now swollen almost twice its normal size. He could feel it throbbing, but strangely, it didn't hurt. That concerned him; however, it was the voice speaking his name, he knew, that was the greatest threat.

"Glad you're able to join us," said the warlord. He was a large man with large hands. His black curly hair was cut so close to the scalp he almost appeared bald. He stood, looking down at Reaper. A smile spread across the man's face as he knelt to bring his face closer to Reaper's. The warlord reached out to touch Reaper's leg. "Hurt a little bit," he said. He poked his finger into the wound, and Reaper struggled to hold back a screech. It hurt, but years of training kept him from screaming out.

"You know it hurts." Reaper's voice didn't sound right. It was raspy and thick. "But that isn't anything new for you, is it? You like to inflict pain."

"Glad you remember me," the warlord responded as he straightened his tall frame.

"Of course, I remember you. You were there when we freed Doc and his family."

Reaper looked around him, and there were his fellow teammates, all except McBeth.

"What have you done with Sergeant Anderson?" he asked.

"Ah, your beloved Sergeant Anderson slipped through my fingers. You see, when I made my deal with Apollo and his friends, I didn't know what I was buying. Only US soldiers is what I asked for, and now look what I have. One of the men that actually came into my camp and stole from me," said the warlord. He began to walk around, kicking the dirt as he moved.

"If it had not been Yassin trying to buy you from me, I would not have known who you are," he added.

"What happened to the sergeant?" repeated Reaper.

The warlord walked over to Reaper and put his foot on his wounded leg. "You better start worrying what is going to happen to you and your teammates," said the warlord, applying pressure on his leg.

This time, Reaper let out a little moan of pain, but he held his composure. He needed to make sure McBeth was still alive.

"Good. You seem to have a high pain tolerance. That will help you over the next couple days. You see, I plan to execute one of you every day. I will show my people and the world, they cannot come into my country and steal from me. No one steals from me," he said, grabbing Reaper by the shoulders, pulling him, and then pushing him down on his back.

"Line the prisoners up," the warlord ordered his men.

The guards grabbed the men and moved them until they were in a straight row. Pressing their knees against the men, they applied pressure. Unable to use their arms to break the fall since their hands were tied behind their backs, the men landed on their knees so that they were kneeling side by side. The warlord paced back and forth in front on the men, who looked back at him defiantly. It didn't matter that all five men were exhausted from the trip from Bucharest to Mali and had no concept of time; they remained defiant. They had no concept of the time or the day. They only knew the sun had climbed higher in the sky, and a lunatic warlord was reveling in the pain of his captives.

The sound of a fire finch alighting on a bush nearby provided a brief respite. Reaper looked over to see a small bird with a red underside and gray wings lift off from a branch and fly toward a rocky hillside visible in a distance. If only he could fly away with that bird, he thought. Instead, his chest tightened, and he thought he was going to be sick again. Heat was crawling up his leg from the injury, and he thought he was probably getting septic. Still, he kept his eyes straight ahead and waited. It didn't take long until the warlord returned to harangue them.

"Several weeks ago, I had something taken from me. Although it wasn't really that important, it was mine, and no one takes anything away from me. You can believe I was surprised to learn that the thieves who had the audacity to steal from me were American soldiers. I know Americans think they control the world, but not here. I am the ruler of this country, and no one takes anything of mine and lives to enjoy it." As the warlord ranted, he walked circles around the bound men.

"I will make examples of these men. The world needs to know to stay away from my country, and my country needs to know I am the law, and I rule with an iron fist," he added, spitting as he talked.

Then, without warning, he stopped behind Martin, drew his pistol, and shot him in the back of the head.

Martin's limp, lifeless body fell facedown in the dirt with his hands still tied behind him.

"You coward son of a bitch!" yelled Reaper, who tried to jerk free. He had seen his friends die in battle but never with a gunshot to the back of their heads while they were bound.

"Oh, don't worry, my friend. I will get to you soon. Each day at sunset, I plan to execute one of you. This man is a nobody to me. He doesn't look like he's even a soldier," said the warlord, who walked over to kick the fallen soldier. Blood was painting the ground around him, seeping into the dirt. The warlord spat again and then turned to stare at Reaper. A wicked grin spread across his face. Reaper just returned the stare, took a deep breath, and then responded.

"He was a soldier, and he was a Marine. He had a family and did nothing to you. Your shooting him the back of the head while he was tied up is a testament to your cowardice. You might like to think you are a somebody, but all I see when I look at you is a bully and a chicken." Surprisingly, Reaper's voice sounded stronger.

Angered by Reaper's reaction, the warlord once again grabbed Reaper's face and said, "Who do you think you are anyway? You are nothing but a thief and a puppet of a capitalistic regime. This is my world, and my people need to know I am in charge. Ever since your soldiers came in here and stole from me, others have thought they could also steal from me and get by with it. Your actions made me look weak to others, and this is no place for weakness of any kind. Even the African Army has attacked me twice, an act for which they will also pay."

"Couldn't happen to a better person," said Reaper through the warlord's squeezing hand.

Dropping his hand from Reaper, the warlord turned to his men. "Take the body to the square as a display for my enemies," said the warlord.

With that said, the warlord ordered his guards to put the prisoners in their cells. The guards grabbed the men and dragged them to outside their cages in the center of the compound. They then threw each one back in with their hands still tied.

"At least untie our hands," said Reaper.

"No need," said the warlord. "I am not concerned with your comfort nor will you live long enough to have to endure it long," he added.

At least in the cage, the men were able to straighten their legs. They attempted to speak to each other, but when they said something, a guard would hit them with a cattle prod. Each time a guard struck them, another guard would laugh. Soon, however, the guards tired of the game, and all but one went to eat.

Inside the cages, the air was stifling, but every now and then, a breeze would blow through. Strangely enough, it was almost like a lullaby. Soon Baylor and Irby were able to fall asleep, but Reaper and

Rogers stayed awake. A single guard walked circles around the caged men nonstop. Reaper and Roger's cages were close enough to whisper to each other when the guard was at his farthest point away.

"Do you have any idea how we got here?" asked Reaper.

"I woke up a couple times, and they hit me with that damn air-needle thing in the neck. Before I passed out, once I saw we were on a boat. Couldn't see any shore, so I guess it was either the Dead Sea or the Mediterranean Sea based on where we were. The next time, we were in wire cages in the back of a truck. I never saw any of the other guys awake, but I'm sure they had the same experience," said Rogers. Rogers was looking rough even though no one would have called him a pretty boy on the best of days.

"We need to get out of here before this lunatic kills us. I sure hope the guys back home decide to come find us. Problem is, we didn't tell anyone where we were or what we were doing," said Reaper.

"Are you the guys that pissed this asshole off?" asked Rogers.

"We are the team that came here and rescued a doctor and his family. I'm guessing that's what he means by 'we stole' from him," continued Reaper. He tried to move his injured leg. Blood had crusted and glued his pant leg to the leg.

Seeing the action, Reaper asked, "How bad is that wound?"

"I think bad, but for now, there is nothing to do about it."

"I'm pretty sure it's infected. Your face is flush with fever."

"I know. I'm pretty sure it's septic." The adrenaline spike Reaper had experienced was gone, and since the warlord wasn't near to him, Reaper's voice now reflected the pain and fatigue he was feeling.

Sensing his friend needed the rest more than he did, Rogers urged him to sleep. "We need to get some rest," said Rogers, trying to get comfortable, squirming around on the ground.

"I've slept enough. We need to figure out a way to get free. Go ahead and rest. I'm betting tomorrow is going to be a long day," said Reaper.

Rogers wanted to argue, but he had been around Reaper enough to know by now that once Reaper decided to do or not to do something, there was little chance of changing his mind.

It didn't take long before Rogers was out. Reaper busied himself studying the compound, counting guards, noting positions, and watching for routines he could take advantage of. Somewhere in the wee hours of the morning, his eyes betrayed him, and he fell asleep. It wasn't long before the rain started then followed by lightening. Two guards gathered under a shed, shielding them from the water. They weren't so concerned with staying dry as they were about betting which one of the metal cages would attract the lightening.

"Make sure you aren't touching the wire cages with any part of your body," said Reaper to the guys.

The rain came down in buckets, and the lightening was criss-crossing across the sky, illuminating the sky so it looked like day-light. The storm raged on for hours, and the ground beneath the guys became mud. Water ran through the compound and started to flow into the cages that were set about a foot deep in the dirt. This had been done to discourage any attempt from the prisoners to try and dig under the bottom of the cages. These cages were not new; they evidently were used by the warlord anytime he wanted to teach someone a lesson. Since the rain came down so hard and so fast, it began to pool inside the cages. Soon the men were forced to stand in the rising waters. Weakened from captivity and still bound, some of them slid back into the mud before finally managing to stand upright. Even though morning finally arrived, the storm kept the sky dark from the rain. It lasted well into the mid part of the day.

"At least we won't die of thirst," said Baylor, always the optimist in the group. He held his face upward and let the rain fall into his mouth.

Reaper was unable to stand too long with his wounded leg. Once he got a good gauge on the extent of the water in his cage, he sat down, with the water only coming mid chest to him. He thought about the wound being in all this contaminated water runoff, but again, it was the least of his worries.

The warlord walked up to the cages to look at the men. Even his olive-green uniform was wet.

"How about some food?" asked Reaper.

"Food. You don't need no stinking food," said the warlord. Obviously, he had watched some old cowboy movies in his time and thought he was funny.

"We're starving," Reaper replied.

"Food should be your last concern. In a few hours, it will be time to demonstrate to my people I am still in charge." He paused and looked at the men he held inside the cages. "You four must choose who dies next," he said and turned to walk away.

"We won't pick. Fuck you," said Reaper.

The warlord stopped and said, "Actually, Sergeant Grimm, you will have to pick." He just laughed after he spoke and turned, walking away, still laughing.

"That's bullshit. I'm not picking anyone," said Reaper, which just caused the warlord to laugh louder.

"We will see," he said, peeking back over his shoulder.

"If that crazy bastard thinks I'm picking someone to die, he's batshit crazy," growled Reaper.

"Bro, he is batshit crazy," answered Baylor. "If you have to pick someone, pick me. All I have is an ex-wife that loves to bust my balls and spend my alimony pay. I'd love to see her face when that meal ticket stops," he added with a faraway grin on his face.

"Hell no, I'm not picking. If someone has to go, it will be me. This wound is getting infected, and I can feel the heat rising through my skin. Without any medic, I'm toast anyway," said Reaper.

"Hold on, guys. I'd like to throw my name in the hat. I think it should be me. Reaper, you got family still alive. Baylor, I love hearing the stories of the crap your ex spends your money on, and Rogers, I don't know you, but you should not have to pay for what we three did here," said Irby.

"You guys are nuts," said Rogers, "but I wouldn't want to be stuck in a cage with anyone else."

All four men laughed at his comment.

"How about we cross that bridge when we get there?" said Reaper.

Although the rain didn't stop for a few more hours, the men spent the time mentally dealing with their own inner demons and preparing themselves for sunset. When the rain did stop, the humidity was unbearable. The coolness of the rain had kept the heat away, but now it was like an oven, baking the men. The day grew shorter, and the sun slowly slipped from the sky.

The warlord came out of whatever place he had been hiding in and walked over to the cages.

"Have you decided who dies?" asked the warlord.

"Yes," quickly answered Reaper to the other men's surprise. "Me," he added. To that, the warlord just grunted.

"No, I am afraid that won't work. You see, I am keeping you until the last man. I want you to witness each of your friend's death before you die. Pick again," he ordered.

"I won't pick," said Reaper.

"You will, and I will tell you why. It is because you care about these men, and you do not want them to suffer. If you don't pick, I will. If I pick, then no easy, painless death like your friend yesterday. I will use my machete and chop off his head. Now, it's not a sharp machete, and it will probably take a few swings to get the job done. It's your choice," said the warlord with an evil grin.

"You bastard. You know I can't pick a man to die. You want it so you can make our deaths as horrible as possible. I'm going to enjoy seeing you die," said Reaper.

"I'm not going to die. Who is going to kill me? You? My people? The African Army? Your beloved America? I don't think so. I am invincible," he said with the look of a lunatic in his eyes.

"Bring the prisoners to the square," said Ntaganda.

The way he said it made it sound like a special place; however, the square was simply a concrete square near the main building of the compound. As the men were being dragged to the square, they passed the pole that held Martin's decapitated head. They hadn't realized that the warlord had chopped off their friend's head. For a few seconds, the men allowed themselves to grieve over the loss of their friend. However, they only allowed themselves brief seconds to do so; they needed to find a way out of this mess.

"Before the week is over, all your heads will be displayed in my courtyard. For all to see, I am in charge and not to test me," sneered Ntganda.

The four men were placed on the concrete square. Again, the guards forced them to kneel with their hands still tied behind their back.

"Have you picked?" the warlord asked Reaper.

Reaper just looked at his buddies and said, "I'm sorry, guys. I just can't do it."

They all mouthed, *It's okay.*

Baylor spoke, "Take me, you psycho bastard. Let's get this done."

"No, take me. This guy wants to die too bad," said Irby, nodding at Baylor.

"I'm not going to make it another day, so if you want your fun with me you, better do it now," said Reaper.

"Don't listen to any of these guys. They weren't even here before. I'm one of the guys that took your doctor," said Rogers, lying through his teeth.

The warlord walked over toward Rogers.

"He's lying. He wasn't on our team and has no idea what happened," said Reaper, trying to get the warlord to walk away from Rogers.

"Oh yeah, then how did I know it was a doctor and his family that was rescued from this sick bastard? All he said to us was that someone was stolen from him," replied Rogers.

The warlord said, "He right. I never said anything about it being the doctor that was stolen. He must be telling the truth."

Reaper started to argue, but the warlord pulled his pistol out of rage and shot Rogers in the forehead out of sheer anger. The small hole where the bullet entered seemed innocuous; however, the back of Rogers's head was lying in small pieces of blood-covered shards and tissue on the ground. Rogers sacrificed had himself for the guys, and they all knew it.

"Take the prisoners back to their cages," said the warlord.

No one spoke as they were dragged-walked back to the cages.

"I didn't know him, but you can damn sure bet I will never forget him as long or short as I live," said Baylor.

The other two men just nodded.

That night, Baylor stayed awake with Reaper.

"You know tomorrow we will have to go through this again," whispered Baylor.

"I know…and he's not going to be tricked into making it quick this time," replied Reaper.

"You are going to have to give him a name, buddy," continued Baylor.

"I just can't sentence a man to death, Rick. I just can't," said Reaper.

"Damn, you just used my first name. I didn't think you knew it." Baylor laughed.

Reaper chuckled under his breath, just loud enough not to attract the guard.

"Let's try and get some rest. We can talk more in the morning," said Reaper.

The men tried to sleep, but the night was cold, and the bugs ate then alive.

"These damn mosquitoes might carry me away through the night, and I won't have to worry about tomorrow," said Reaper, using his chin to smash a quarter-size mosquito on his neck.

Baylor laughed and rolled over to rest.

The next morning came with a lot of commotion. The guards were running around the compound. No one seemed to be in control, and since neither Reaper nor Baylor had rested, they watched the scene unfold.

"Are you awake, princess?" Baylor whispered to Irby.

"Yes, but I think I lost a pint of blood to these damn bugs," replied Irby.

"What's going on?" asked Baylor.

"Not sure, but they look like they have seen a ghost the way they are running around like chickens with their heads cut off," said Reaper.

Baylor pointed in the opposite direction. The warlord was headed their way. Once he neared their cages, he began to speak, "Looks like we have a little treat in store for you today."

"What, you decided to surrender or, better yet, kill yourself?" quipped Baylor.

"No, we have a visitor for this evening's show, and we are going to broadcast it on the Internet," said the warlord. "Now the rest of the world will see I am still in charge here and not to challenge my rule."

The day sped by for the three men. Near starvation, their bodies were shutting down. Soon It was close to sunset.

"Okay, here's how we are going to do this. Reaper, think of a number between one and twenty. Don't say it out loud. Thomas and I will pick our numbers, and the closest wins," suggested Baylor.

"It's still making me pick, and I can't," said Reaper.

"You have to," said Irby.

"Okay, Thomas, guess how old Reaper is," said Baylor.

"Twenty-eight." said Irby

"I guess twenty-nine," said Baylor. "How old are you, Reaper? And it's not you choosing. It's us deciding," he added.

"I'm thirty," answered Reaper, lowering his head.

"Great, I win. So when Mr. Hairy nose asks who you pick, you say me," continued Baylor.

"I don't know if I can, Rick," said Reaper.

"Bro, if you don't, one of us is getting hacked to death on the Internet. I don't want my ex to see that. She might enjoy it too much. And Thomas has a mom and dad still alive. They don't need to see their boy go out that way. You say you can't choose, but I'm saying you are helping us by just saying what we just decided," preached Baylor.

"Okay, Rick, I will do it, but it's against my will, and you know that," said a teary-eyed Reaper.

"And the next day, there's no worries either. It will just be me," said Irby.

Reaper looked away from his friends to see the warlord and his guard approaching the cages. Two other men followed. Reaper recognized one of them. It was Yassin; the other man was draped in black with a hood covering his face.

"Glad to see you're still kicking, Sergeant. How's the leg?" asked Yassin.

"Screw you," replied Reaper.

"I couldn't talk Ntaganda into selling you to me, but he did invite me to his little show tonight. I sure hope you are the main attraction," said Yassin.

"Hey, if the sick bastard wants to put me on the Internet, so be it," replied Reaper.

"Stick to the plan," said Baylor. The guard closest to him tapped him with the cattle prod.

"No, the sergeant will be the last to die, but tonight should be entertaining, watching them squirm to pick the prisoner to be executed," said the warlord. "Bring the prisoners to the square," he ordered the guards.

The guards took the three men to the concrete square. An empty pole stood next to Martin's and Roger's display.

"Ready for a little fun?" said the warlord to Yassin.

"Who will you pick tonight?" he asked Reaper, nudging Yassin with his elbow.

"Corporal Baylor," said Reaper to Ntaganda's surprise.

"Wait, no arguing, no 'he said this, he said that.' This is no fun, but at least it is settled," said the warlord, walking over to Baylor.

But this time, he didn't pull out his pistol. He pulled out his machete.

"You said if I chose, you would make it quick!" screamed Reaper.

"Who wants to see a simple shooting on the Internet? A good beheading will get me the recognition I deserve," said the warlord.

He looked at his guards and said, "Start the broadcast."

The guard behind the camera gave the warlord a thumbs-up.

"Yassin, would you and your friend like to join me on camera?" asked the warlord.

Yassin spoke to the hooded friend, and he shook his head no.

"I think we will let you have all the glory today, my friend," responded Yassin.

The warlord started his speech about the Americans and how they stole from him. But Reaper was lost in the moment, concerned for Baylor. Baylor just yawned like he was getting bored and wanted the show to get going.

Finally, Ntaganda said, "You have been found guilty of trying to overthrow my regime, and for this, I sentence you to death by beheading." He raised his machete high over his head, but before he could swing down, a shot rang out.

CHAPTER 10

Party Favors

McBeth sat quietly in her chair and watched the young girls put on their party dresses and fix their makeup. Amelia was struggling to keep from crying, but no one wanted Cindy to pay the price of their actions. Amelia had a beautiful light-blue chiffon dress and a hair ribbon that matched. All the girls looked like little dolls. All except poor Cindy; she wore only a makeshift hospital gown, and her hair was matted and tangled. The guard made sure she had regular showers, but by the look of it, she was never given anything to wear.

McBeth wondered what had happened to give this young girl the scar that put her in the whipping-post position of the group.

"Okay, pretty ladies, it's time to party," said one of the guards. "I want you to be on your best behavior, and no crying around the clients."

He walked over to Cindy and grabbed a big handful of hair, pulling it back so far it almost snapped her neck. The girls let out a "please don't," but Cindy didn't even flinch. Her eyes appeared glazed over as she retreated into her private world where nothing touched her. By now, she was so accustomed to the abuses she had become almost numb to the pain and had figured out a way to escape. All she had to do was sink into herself and ignore what was happening. Sometimes the pain was so great it pulled her back to reality, but more and more, she was fading away into that safe place where nothing could touch her.

The guard didn't even seem to notice that Cindy had retreated into herself; he just looked at the others and reminded them,

"Remember what happens if you cause any problems or don't cooperate with our clients." He finished his comments and released Cindy's hair. Walking away from her, he signaled to the other girls and ordered them to follow him, and they walked single file out the cell. Left in the room were McBeth, who was tied to a chair, and Cindy, who had disappeared into herself.

"Sweetheart, can you hear me?" asked McBeth but received no reaction from Cindy.

"Cindy," said McBeth, a little stronger.

For a few minutes, Cindy didn't respond, but then she shifted her eyes toward McBeth. When McBeth saw Cindy's eyes, she caught her breath. She had seen that thousand-yard stare of the lights before in others whose physical presence remained, but no one was home.

"Cindy, sweetheart, can you hear me?" she tried one more time.

Again, no response. This poor young girl just continued to stare blindingly into space.

A guard stepped in the room and looked at McBeth.

"I said no talking. Do I need to make my point clearer than that?" he said, looking at Cindy.

McBeth responded, "I'm sorry. Please. I will be quiet."

The guard pointed at McBeth. "Lights out. I don't want any noise coming out of this room. You hear me," he stated.

McBeth just nodded yes, and Cindy laid back on her bed.

For what seemed hours, McBeth sat quietly in the chair. In the dark, she occasionally got a glimpse of Cindy when a guard would pass the door, and his flashlight sent shards of light into the room. Cindy just laid on the bed, staring at the ceiling.

Eventually, the metal door opened, and the guard flipped the lights on. The young girls were returning. They walked in the same as they walked out, except they were one short. Amelia wasn't with the returning girls. McBeth's heart started to race, and she sat up from her semi-slouched position in the chair. You could see the look in the girl's eyes. McBeth knew not to start asking questions or even talk in front of the guards.

The remaining girls took off their party dresses and neatly put them back in the storage boxes. Then together they went into the shower to wash away their makeup. Over time, they had learned to all go at once because water was only turned on for a shorth length of time, allowing the showers. After they all showered, dressed for bed, and crawled into their bunks, the guard turned off the lights and left the room. But he didn't leave before stroking Cindy's head and saying, "I guess no party tonight, but tomorrow is another day." His hand rubbed across Cindy's head, and he pulled her hair at the last touch. As he left the room, he turned the lights off.

When the door closed, one of the girls looked at McBeth and just put her finger to her lips to keep her quiet. After a few minutes, a faint voice in the dark spoke.

"Amelia was sold tonight," said the voice with a slight crack in her voice.

"To whom?" asked McBeth.

"We never know their names. Sometimes they wear suits. Sometimes it's just robes, but I've even seen uniforms. No names ever, and we aren't allowed to ask," replied the voice.

That poor girl, thought McBeth.

"We have to sit on their laps, listen to their jokes, and pretend to have a good time," continued the voice.

"If we don't, we end up like Cindy," said another voice in the dark.

"What happened to Cindy?" asked McBeth.

"Cindy was sitting on some fat Russian's lap, and she accidently spilled her champagne on his pants. He backhanded her as she took a drink, and the glass broke, cutting her face. It was bad. She bled on her party dress and the client's suit. They brought her back and sewed up her face, leaving that nasty scar. Now, since she has the scar, she can't be sold. They use her to keep us in line. If we mess up, well, you saw what happens. They like it when we mess up," said the tiny voice.

"There was another girl here before Cindy. When they started with Cindy, they took the other girl out, and we never saw her again," whimpered one of the girls.

McBeth tried to see each of the girls as they huddled beneath their blankets. They were so little, she thought, so little and fragile and yet their strength was admirable. Even though what they were experiencing what had to be frightening and painful, their concern for each other and for Cindy overcame their fears. Now that the day was over and they settled in their beds, they, too, escaped into a world of their own making, where nothing or no one could touch them.

"We need to stick together. People will be looking for me, and they will come and get us all," stated McBeth. She wasn't sure any of the girls heard her, but a small voice responded.

"I hope so," one of the girls spoke but immediately stopped talking as a guard opened the door.

CHAPTER 11

RAID ON THE WARLORD

Ntaganda, the warlord, stumbled back, his right arm gone from mid forearm down. Baylor fell onto his face, away from the staggering warlord, with Reaper and Irby following suit. All hell broke loose. The guard towers exploded and crumbled down onto the compound, sending a hailstorm of debris into the air. The warlord's men were running around, firing frantically into the hillside. Short machine-gun fire erupted from the hillside followed by RPGs. Vehicles in the compound exploded with such force the ground shook and knocked the warlord's men off their feet.

During the chaos, Yassin and his hooded friend reached their armored Humvee and maneuvered their vehicle through the gauntlet of fire and the debris.

"Someone hit that Humvee with a rocket!" called out Smitty.

One of the rebels heard Smitty's cry and lowered his sights on the zigzagging vehicle. Right before he fired, he saw a truck bringing more soldiers into the compound and chose that as his target, letting the Humvee slip out of range and through the fingers of the assault team.

The rocket zoomed in on its target, and the truck disappeared in a puff of white and red smoke.

"Sorry, my friend, but I figured the truck was a better target," said the racketeer.

"I agree," replied Amir, and he slapped the man on the back and got back into the fight.

The warlord gathered his composure and wrapped a makeshift tourniquet around his arm, stopping the bleeding. He had many

McBETH

times used this method in stopping the bleeding of those he cut their arms off, just to prolong their deaths. Seeing that his prisoners were still on the ground before him, he reached across his waist and tugged on his pistol with his left hand. However, the holster was reluctant to release the weapon from Ntaganda's attempted cross-hand draw. He stood there, tugging at his holster and screaming orders to his remaining men.

Cap had Amir and ten men working their way toward the compound from the southwest corner of the compound. Smitty and Bain took ten men and worked their way in from the southeast corner. MK and a spotter set up a sniper nest on the hillside on the west side, with Snyder doing the same from the east side. Murph and Bruce covered the north end of the compound and took out anyone that tried to slip through.

One of the warlord's men ran to him and helped him get his pistol free from his holster. Just as he started to hand the pistol to the warlord, his head exploded in a pink mist. MK chambered another round, still looking at the warlord through his scope.

"Do I have a green light on the warlord?" asked MK.

"No," said Cap. "We still don't know where a couple of our people are. And if they aren't here, he may know, so we need him alive," he added.

The warlord bent over to pick up the pistol, but MK fired another round and took off Ntaganda's left hand, right at the wrist. The warlord let out a fierce scream and sat down on the concrete square, feet from the three men he planned to execute.

Seeing their leader in a position of surrender, the remainder of the warlord's men started dropping their weapons and raising their hands in the air.

"Cease-fire, cease-fire," ordered Cap to the team.

The two approaching teams from the corners of the compound met just in front of the concrete square.

"Amir, check our people and try not to let that bastard die until I talk to him," said Cap.

Amir went straight to Reaper and checked him out. Smitty cut Baylor and Irby loose and helped them stand.

103

"You guys okay?" asked Smitty.

"I could sure use a drink," answered Baylor.

Smitty pulled out his flask and handed it to Baylor, who took a big swig and handed it to Irby, who did the same. Baylor handed the flask back to Smitty with a thankful smile.

"Where is everyone else?" asked Cap.

"Cap, he killed Rogers and Martin," answered Baylor.

"What about McBeth?" Cap asked.

"She didn't come with us. From what I gathered from the warlord, she was sold to someone else. He didn't know who we were until that fucking Yassin asshole told him," replied Baylor.

"He keeps resurfacing every time something bad is going on. The next time I see him..." was as far as Cap got when Baylor interrupted.

"You just missed him. He and his buddy ran out of here when the entire melee started," said Baylor.

"That must have been him in the Humvee that slipped out when the troop truck arrived," said Amir.

Cap stepped over to Amir treating Reaper.

"How's he doing, Doc?" asked Cap.

"He's lost a lot of blood, and his leg is infected," replied Amir. "We need to get him somewhere safe if I am going to save his leg and his life," he added.

"Well, that isn't this place," said Murph.

"Clearing the buildings and working our way to you, we came across the radio room. The radio operator got a message out to the diamond mine. According to the operator's last words, the general is coming with fifty men," reported Murph.

"Can he travel?" Cap asked Amir.

"He will have to be carried," replied Amir.

"That's no problem," said MK, joining the team. He handed his rifle to Snyder and lifted Reaper slowly onto his feet and picked him up in the standard fireman's carry.

Cap smiled at MK and turned to the rest of the team.

"We need to roll out of here. Get all your guys together and meet us in the clearing just south of here," said Cap.

Amir's friends gathered up their weapons and a few extra and headed to the rally point.

"What do you want to do with him?" said Smitty, pointing at the warlord.

"You can run, you can hide, but eventually, I will find you," said Ntaganda to Cap and Smitty.

"And you," he said, pointing to Amir. "I will find your family, and they will pay for your defiance."

The team looked around, and Amir said, "You men go ahead. I will make sure the warlord's bleeding stops. I am a physician, and it is my duty." What he said astonished the team.

"You can't be serious," said Baylor. "He just threatens your family and to hunt us all down. I don't know about you, but I don't like looking over my shoulders all the time."

"I can't leave him bleeding to death," replied Amir. "Please do as I asked."

"Come on, guys, let's do what the doc asked," said Smitty.

The team headed out of the compound and into the trees. They had gone about one hundred yards when they heard a single gunshot. They paused for a minute, worried about Amir, but their fears subsided when they saw him running to meet up with them.

"What happened?" asked Cap.

"I stopped the bleeding," said Amir, and he trotted past the team, headed to the clearing.

When the team reached the rally point, Amir's friends were all waiting. The small shrubs and wildflowers disappeared and left the team exposed. The group rested for a minute, planning their route out of the warlord's lands and back into the safe area of Mauritania.

Amir took point, and the rest of the team followed. Baylor pointed to Amir.

"Isn't that the same doc that we rescued from the warlord?" asked Baylor

"It sure is," responded Murph.

"Someone is going to have to explain to me what the hell is going on," said a confused Baylor.

"It's a long story. One we can tell on the plane ride home," answered Smitty.

The group traveled for about three klicks when Amir stopped.

"We have to get over that ridge. On the other side is Mauritania. My friends are going to head east and go back to their villages," reported Amir.

The men all shook hands and parted ways. Amir led the DOG team toward the ridge. They had barely moved when machine-gun fire started raining down on the team's position. The team took cover behind some large rocks but had no way of seeing where the fire was coming from.

"See if you can work your way back down the ridge a bit and circle around," Cap ordered Snyder.

"I'll go with you," said Smitty, and the two started to slip between rocks, working their way down.

Just as they cleared the rocks, they were met by small-arms fire from a truck sitting at the bottom of the ridge. They ducked at the last minute. Seeing there was no route down and around, they worked their way back to the team.

"Back door is closed," said Smitty. "There's a truck full of bad guys waiting on us to come back that way."

No sooner than Smitty had talked, a booming voice sounded. "This is General Djenno Hombori. I am the new commander-in-chief of the Mali Freedom Army. You will lay down your weapons and surrender immediately," said a voice over a loudspeaker.

"Boy, these guys work fast getting a new commander," said Smitty.

"This General Hombori has wanted power for years. He is the one that has done all the old warlord's bidding. Probably crazier than the warlord," stated Amir.

"That's great. Out of the frying pan and into the fire," said Bain.

The team sat there for several minutes, considering their options.

"Surrender isn't an option," said Cap. "This idiot will just finish what the old one started but have more heads to chop off," he continued.

"We can't call for help, so what do we do?" said Murph.

Cap remembered the conversation with the president. *We can't come to your rescue, but I will give you a number to use in case of an emergency*, he remembered.

Cap reached in the front pocket of his vest and pulled out his sat phone. He retrieved the number and pushed the digits.

"Hello," said a rough Russian voice on the phone.

"I was given this number and told if I need help to call it," answered Cap.

"Who gives you dis number?" said the voice.

"A mutual friend. She said you could help us," replied Cap, not saying who gave the number but definitely a clue.

"Ah, she said I might be hearing from you," said the voice. "So what can I do for you?"

"We are in a nice little crossfire with no way of getting out without a lot of casualties," said Cap.

"I'm looking at your GPS location and bringing you up on satellite," said the Russian.

Smitty just looked at Cap and mouthed the word, *Satellite!*

"Who the hell is that?" whispered Smitty to Cap.

Cap just shook his head and stayed on the phone.

"Okay, I have you. Yes, you are in a mess. I count twenty-five to thirty men above and below you," he stated.

"The new commander of the MFA, General Hombori, is above us and is demanding we surrender," informed Cap.

"What has happened to the warlord Ntaganda?" asked the Russian.

"He retired," answered Cap.

The Russian let out a big laugh and said, "He needed to retire years ago, but this Hombori is no general. He is a butcher. Let me see what I can do. Please hold."

Cap pulled the phone down from his face and looked at Smitty. "He put me on hold, and it's terrible Russian music playing," he said.

Cap took the time to take his team's measure. Baylor, Grimm, and Irby looked rough, but not in danger. However, Reaper had passed out, and his skin was pale and glossy. He was getting to check with Amir about Reaper's status when the Russian spoke.

"I am back. In about five minutes, you will see an opening to go up the ridge. Make sure you move when you see the opportunity," said the Russian, and he hung up.

"Wait," said Cap, but the Russian was gone. He tried to call the number back, but it was a dead line now.

"What did he say?" asked Smitty as the team listened in.

"He said, in five minutes, we will see our opportunity to go up the ridge. He said he must move when we see it," explained Cap as the team poised themselves for the opportunity.

Cap looked at his watch and said, "Thirty seconds. Get ready."

In a few minutes, a low roar was heard in the air. Then up from the other side of the ridge was a dark-grey drone. The drone passed over the men and fired rockets into the hillside above them.

"I think that's our sign. Let's go!" shouted Cap, and the team started working their way up the ridge to the top.

The drone made another pass below them and lit up the area behind them. A large fireball appeared when the troop truck exploded.

The team reached the top of the ridge and looked down into Mauritania.

"We are safe now," said Amir, pointing to the river.

"We still need to get Reaper some medical attention. And I mean fast," said Smitty.

"MK, you okay carrying him?" asked Cap.

"You know what they say. He ain't heavy, he's my brother," replied MK as he started down the other side of the ridge.

The team worked their way down to the river and crossed over into Mauritania. Once across the river, Amir had trucks waiting to carry the team back to the airfield.

Amir treated Reaper in route but voiced his concerns to Cap.

"Cap, he really looks bad. I don't know if I can save the leg," said Amir. "I'm afraid the infection is in his blood. He's looking very jaundiced. I need to get a medical facility quick so I can start an IV. I don't have my portable infusion pump with me."

Cap looked at Reaper and said, "Buddy, we may have to take your leg to save your life. Is that what you want us to do?"

At some point during the retreat, Reaper had regained consciousness. He looked at Cap and shook his head no.

"Doc, do what you can. We will be at the airstrip in a few minutes, and we can get him better situated there. We have a portable IV pump onboard with our other equipment," said Cap.

A few minutes later, the truck pulled up to a waiting plane and two anxious ladies.

"Did you get them. Are they all right?" asked Callie.

"Reaper's hurt bad, and there was no sign of McBeth. We lost two of Reapers team to the warlord," answered Cap. He motioned for the women to move out of the way. "We need to get Reaper in the plane and the IV started." He signaled for Smitty to carry Reaper ahead of the others.

"Once we are on the plane, let's take off. I don't know how much time the Russian has bought us."

Smitty carried Reaper onto the plane and made him as comfortable as possible. Callie unpacked the portable IV pump and other medical supplies. She handed them to Amir, who immediately began working on Reaper.

Callie joined Michelena in the cockpit and started takeoff procedures.

"Cap, where are we going?" asked Michelena.

"We need to get Reaper to a hospital quick," said Cap.

"I think the closest military base is the Naval Station Rota, Spain," replied Michelena.

"Then that's where we are going," said Cap as he picked up his sat phone.

He dialed the number, and Rebolini picked up on the other end.

"What's the news?" asked Rebolini.

"Reaper is wounded and needs immediate medical attention. We are airborne headed toward Spain to the naval base there. Can you get us clearance?" said Cap.

"I'll make the call. What about the rest of the team?" asked Rebolini.

"We lost Martin and Rogers. McBeth is still missing," he replied.

"Copy that," said Rebolini, and he hung up the phone and called the president.

"What are we going to do about McBeth?" asked Smitty. "Anyone who might know where she is, is dead."

"Not everyone. Remember when we were talking to Apollo," asked Cap.

"Yes, but he lied about where she was," said Smitty.

"He wasn't the only one there," replied Cap.

"Eurie," said Smitty.

"Yes, he said he didn't know, but he knew where Apollo kept his records," said Cap.

"What makes you think he will help us?" asked Smitty.

"He and I bonded. He will help," said Cap.

The plane flew into Spanish airspace and was given permission to land at the naval base. After taxiing down the runway, they were met with military and emergency vehicles. Reaper was loaded into an ambulance and taken to the base hospital. The rest of the team were escorted to a nearby hanger. In the hanger, the team was met by an officer.

"Good evening. My name is Clifford Lee. I have been ordered to assist your team with any necessities," said the lieutenant.

"Nice to meet you, sir," said Cap. "I need a videoconferencing room and a direct line to Washington," he added.

"Follow me," said the lieutenant, leading Cap to a room connected to the hanger. Inside the room were video screens and computers.

"I'm sure you can make your call from here," said the lieutenant, leaving the room.

Cap used the phone and called JJ at the main office. He instructed him to work his magic and set up a video call to Rebolini. In just a few minutes, the video screen came alive, and there stood Rebolini in the command center with the president and the general.

"Good evening," said the president.

"Good evening," replied Cap, who was joined by Smitty in the conference room.

"Tell us what's going on," said the president.

"We were able to rescue Grimm, Baylor, and Irby. We lost Martin and Rogers. We still don't know where Sergeant Anderson is being held, but we have a good lead," reported Cap.

"I understand you were also able to find the sergeant's niece and a couple other young ladies," stated the president.

"Yes, ma'am. It seems these girls were taken and being sold in Europe and Asia," responded Cap.

"Were they all Americans?" asked the general.

"No, sir. Two were Americans, two were English, and the fifth was from France," answered Cap.

"Just so you know: they are all safe in London, and we flew the sergeant's sister there to be re-united with her daughter," said the president.

"What do you need to follow up on your lead on McBeth?" asked Rebolini.

"I'm going to take one person and go back to Constanta to take a look at the syndicate's records," answered Cap.

The president looked directly at Cap. "Not a lot we can do to help you, and I'm sorry," she said.

"We understand," replied Cap.

The president looked at someone else who was in the room, but unseen by Cap and Smitty. Seeming to come to some type of decision, she again spoke to Cap.

"What we can do is make sure your team is well taken care of and your wounded teammate gets medical treatment," said the president.

"If you can make sure they all have clearance at the naval base in Spain so they can visit with Reaper and get some rest, that will be enough for now. Three of our men also need medical attention. I plan to leave within the hour to…" Cap stopped speaking. "I'm sure you don't need to know those details, and oh, by the way, the number came in handy," said Cap with a smile.

The call ended, and Smitty said, "You know I'm going with you."

"I wouldn't have it any other way," said Cap.

Cap and Smitty returned to the team.

"Cap and I are going back to talk to Eurie. He knows where Apollo kept his records, and I think we can persuade him to let us look at any hard copies stored there," said Smitty to the group.

"We need to keep it small not to attract any attention to us," said Cap to the team, seeing they weren't happy being left behind.

"I want you guys ready to move on a minute's notice. As soon as we get the info from Eurie, I don't want any delays," stated Cap, focusing their attention back on the task at hand. "You will have clearance to stay at the naval lodge. The president is already making the arrangements. I need you to rest so that once we know where McBeth is, you are ready to leave." He turned his attention to Grimm, Baylor, and Irby. "You three will report to the hospital there to be checked out."

Baylor held up his hand, and Grimm began to speak, but Cap headed them off.

"I know, I know... You are big, tough guys who think you are invincible. I want to remind you that you almost died. You won't do us or McBeth any good if you are too tired or sick to help us. Go to the hospital, get checked out, eat some food, go to bed, and for God's sake, take a bath. You stink." The last comment earned him a laugh.

While Cap spoke, Amir had been quietly listening. Now, however, he stood up and said, "I would like to go check on Reaper."

"Me too," said Callie

Cap called the lieutenant who arranged for their transportation to the base hospital.

"Lieutenant, you don't happen to know if the Navy has any carriers near the coast of Bulgaria, do you?" asked Cap.

CHAPTER 12
RUSSIAN/NORTH KOREAN LINE

The pilot radioed ahead for clearance to land. The towered responded in confirmation. The light-gray C-2 Greyhound slowly made its descent out of the clouds over the Black Sea.

"Tighten your straps, boys. When that cable grabs the plane, you might lose a tooth or two," said the pilot with a slight chuckle.

The copilot looked at the pilot. "Not sure what connection these guys have, but having the US government fly just the two of them all the way here must be high up," he said.

"Definitely above our pay grade," said the pilot.

As the C-2 broke out of the clouds, they could see their landing strip ahead.

"*Gipper*, this is Greyhound C-2. We see you and are lined up for approach," said the pilot over the radio.

"Copy, C-2. We see you, and you have permission to approach and descend," responded the voice on the radio.

The C-2 slowly descended toward the target.

"C-2, this is *Gipper*. Drop to 3000 and maintain course," said the voice on the radio.

"Copy, Gipper, dropping to 3000," responded the pilot.

"C-2, this is *Gipper*, at vector 2564, descend for landing. C-2 has the ball," said the voice on the radio.

"Copy, *Gipper*, descend at vector 2564, and we have the ball," responded the pilot.

"Okay, guys, this is it. Get ready for one hell of a ride," said the copilot to Cap and Smitty.

The Greyhound slowed and got lower and lower toward the water. Cap looked out the window across from him and thought, *Is this damn plane landing on the water?* He got his answer a split second later when the plane's wheels touched down on the flight deck of the *USS Ronald Reagan*. The plane hit the deck a little harder than a normal landing, and milliseconds later, the plane literally came to a complete stop. It was so fast, for a minute, the guys were thrown forward so hard they became weightless in their seats.

"Welcome to the *USS Ronald Reagan,* gentlemen," said the copilot.

The *USS Ronald Reagan CVN-76* is a Nimitz-class, nuclear-powered carrier. It's home to over three thousand personnel and is based out of Yokosuka Naval Base in Japan.

The pilot and copilot came back from the cockpit and helped Cap and Smitty out of their harnesses. Smitty's sleeves were rolled up, and they got a glimpse of his SEAL tattoo on his bicep.

"Not sure what you boys got going on, but we wish you Godspeed and a safe return," said the veteran pilot.

"Thank you, sir, and we appreciate the ride," said Smitty with a quick salute.

The doors to the plane opened, and a couple soldiers came into the plane.

"Sir, we are here to assist you during your stay on the *Gipper. Gipper* is the nickname of the *USS Ronald Reagan,*" said the soldier to Smitty.

"We are supposed to meet with Master Chief Burton when we arrive," said Smitty to the soldiers.

"Yes, sir. He is waiting in one of the bays for you two," replied the soldier as they grabbed the two bags that Cap and Smitty brought. The group exited the plane and proceeded to the bay where a few men were waiting.

"You look like shit, Smitty," said the master chief as they approached the waiting men.

"Damn, you got old since I saw you last," replied Smitty to the master chief.

The two men looked at each other for a minute.

"Men look at me that way for only two reasons," said the master chief. "They either want to fight me or fuck me."

Cap was too savvy to misinterpret the looks being exchanged. Only pals who had been through hell and back together formed that kind of bond. Cap stepped to the side and watched as Smitty and the Master Chief responded together, "And I'm all out of condoms." The two men broke into laughter and gave each other a huge bear hug.

"Damn glad to see ya, boy. How have you been? I see you haven't missed any meals," said the master chief patting Smitty on the belly.

"I'm good, sir. I figured you would have had enough of this man's Navy and retired," responded Smitty.

"Five months, two weeks, one day, and a wake-up." The master chief smiled.

"Oh, Master Chief, this is Malcolm Rodgers. Cap, this is Master Chief Andre Burton, one of the craziest SOBs I've ever had the privilege to serve with," said Smitty.

Cap reached out his hand and shook the master chief's.

"It's a pleasure to meet you, Master Chief," responded Cap.

"So what you boys got going on, and why isn't my team involved?" asked the master chief.

"Just some recon and intel gathering," responded Smitty. His short, prepared answered caused the master chief's eyebrow to raise.

"Intel gathering," sarcastically said the master chief. "What the hell does that un-politically, correctly mean?" he added.

"One of our friends is missing. Marine Sergeant Mckenzie Anderson. We have good info that a man in Constanta will know where we can find her," explained Smitty.

"Missing Marine. Why are they using you guys to locate her? No offense, but it should be a military matter," responded the master chief.

"She went missing after taking a leave of absence to find her missing niece. She and a small force entered Romania illegally and were captured. Turns out, the group that captured her team were a bunch of human smugglers. We were able to rescue and recover the other members, but she is still missing," informed Cap.

"Recovered?" asked the master chief.

"Yes, two of her team were killed by an African warlord," answered Smitty.

"And what's his status?" asked the master chief.

"Retired," responded Smitty.

"Let me get this straight. As I see it, her team got pinched, slipping into Romania, and they were sold to other buyers by these smugglers? Our government doesn't want to look like the bad guys here and go in and get them, so they are sending your team to do their dirty work. And we are here to help you…unofficially," said the master chief.

"In defense of the administration, we originally thought it was the Romanian government that captured the team, and the president didn't want an international incident with our soldiers invading Romania," responded Cap.

"Okay, but now they know it's not a government but a group of human traffickers. We should be going instead of you guys," replied the master chief, getting his feathers ruffled.

"I understand exactly what you are saying, Master Chief, but the two of us have a history with the man we are going to see. And if it goes south, it's just two guys in the wrong place at the wrong time," said Smitty.

The master chief paused for a minute. "Which one of you is the boyfriend?" he asked.

"Excuse me," responded Cap, looking at Smitty.

"No, I don't mean between you two. I mean with Sergeant Anderson," he explained.

Smitty just rolled his eyes in direction of Cap. Cap was just looking at the master chief with his "screw you" eyes.

"What do you guys need from me?" asked the master chief, getting back on the subject.

"We just need a boat," said Cap.

"Our original plan was to get to Varna, Bulgaria, then work our way up the coast to Constanta," said Smitty.

"So you want to go to Varna or Constanta?" asked the master chief.

"Ultimately, Constanta," answered Cap. "But we were worried travelling that distance in a boat on open waters."

"You guys hit the jackpot landing here on the *Gipper*. We happened to have onboard one of the finest ultralight mini subs in the fleet. SOFREP's SMX-26 SDVs," bragged the master chief. "We can drop you at the docks in Constanta, and no one would ever see us."

"What is an SDV?" asked Smitty.

"SEAL delivery vehicle. The SDV is a dry mini, which makes a longer trip easier and more comfortable. It allows us to save our breathing air for when we get close to the target," explained the master chief.

Cap looked at Smitty. "I like your friends," he said. "When can we launch?"

"It will take about sixty minutes to prep. We will be ready in sixty-one," replied the master chief.

"We also will need a little firepower, just in case," said Smitty.

"No problem. We have a good supply of that too," responded the master chief.

"Take these men to supply cabinet, and I'll get the ball rolling on the SDV," ordered the master chief.

True to his word. In sixty-one minutes, the SDV hit the water in route to Constanta. In the sub was Cap, Smitty, Master Chief, and one other SEAL.

"We have about two hours of travel time unless we have any issues," said the master chief.

"Issues?" asked Cap.

"We are traveling into the territorial waters of other countries in a US vehicle. I'm not sure what level of cooperation their Navy will give us if we are caught, so we are taking it easy and avoiding any regular shipping routes," answered the master chief.

"I'll just sit back and let you guys do your thing," said Cap, lowering his cap down over his eyes.

The master chief and his officer went about their task of avoiding any ships and staying away from land for almost two hours.

"I have the LZ in sight," said the master chief. "Don your wet gear and get ready to deploy."

Cap and Smitty put on their gear and went into the dive chamber of the mini sub.

"I'll fill the chamber and open the hatch. When you get the green light, deploy," said the master chief.

"Bring our girl home," he said to Cap, tapping him on his air tank.

Master Chief shut the door, and the water began to fill the chamber. A hatch below them opened slowly, and they sat, waiting for the dive light to change from red to green.

The water was cold, but they stayed focused on the light. Soon it changed to green, and they slipped off their bench and down through the hatch. As soon as they cleared the hatch, it began to close. The SDV turned and headed away from them in the murky port water. Smitty and Cap worked their way to the support pole for the pier and rose slowly out of the water. Their heads broke surface to find there was a torrential rainstorm on land.

"Lucky break," said Smitty. "We can use the storm to get out of the water undetected."

"Eurie's house isn't far from here either. Your buddies sure know how to sneak around," said Cap.

"Hey, it's what SEALs do, brother: sneak in, perform the job, and get out before anyone even knows they are there," replied Smitty.

"There's a ladder over there near that barge. We will use it to get out of the water. Doesn't look like anyone has been on that thing in years." reported Cap.

The two men swam over to the ladder and tied their tanks on a long leash, letting them sink out of sight but available for their return. They then worked their way up the ladder onto the barge.

"We need to get off this barge and out of the port," informed Cap.

The two lowered themselves over the edge of the barge onto the dock. Then they worked their way to an area behind some large cargo containers. When they removed their wet suits, they felt the full impact of the freezing rain from the storm. Each man had brought a coat, hat, and gloves in anticipation of the cold weather, but nothing for the rain. With their weapons tucked under their coats, they stepped out from behind the cargo containers and saw a man running toward the front gate of the dock area they were in. While the man was running, he raised his hand and waved at a man in a glass tower overlooking the pier. The man raised the gate, and the man ran through and straight out of the port area.

Cap looked at Smitty and said, "Follow me," and the two men started running toward the gate. When they reached the point where the other man waved, they started doing the same. On cue, the gate opened, and they ran through and out of the port area.

"I hate the rain, but it was our friend today. I hope our pal Eurie is home," said Smitty.

The rain was still pouring around them, so the two men walked at a brisk pace; their heads lowered as they attempted to avoid the puddles forming on the sidewalk.

For a few minutes, they continued walking until they passed the road to the bazaar and approached Eurie's house. It was a small, two-story structure set back from the road. Even though it appeared well-kept, the rain was coming down so hard it gushed from the gutters.

"I'll take the back and you the front. Let's hope he doesn't have any quests. The rain will mask any sounds we make, so it should be easy to gain entrance if no one answers the front door," said Smitty as he cut around the block to the back of Eurie's place.

Cap waited a couple minutes to let Smitty get in place, and he walked up to the front door and knocked. A woman opened the door, which surprised Cap.

"Is Eurie home?" he asked.

The woman paused before answering. "I'm not sure. What business do you have with my brother?" Her English was perfect, with just a slight accent.

"We are old friends?" he answered.

Just then, Smitty came walking through the hallway with Eurie by the arm.

"Somebody decided to slip out the back door," said Smitty.

"Eurie, I thought we were friends," said Cap as he stepped into the doorway.

"You men cannot come into my house uninvited and start pushing us around," said the woman. Although she was a short woman, her hips and bust were well rounded. She used that size to attempt blocking Cap from moving closer into the house.

Afraid his sister might get hurt in any ensuring melee, Eurie turned to her and said, "Please, sister, these are my old friends. I thought they were someone else coming here to harm me."

"Friends! Huh," said the woman, walking away and toward a window on the side wall. She leaned against the wall, facing them, and folded her arms around her waist. "You must think me a fool if you think I believe these men are your friends. Look at them. They wear suits, but beneath them, I can see the outline of weapons." The rain had caused both men's jackets to stick their frames and, in so doing, clearly outline the weapons they carried.

"Izzie," Eurie repeated, "I promise you that these men mean me no harm. If they wanted to kill me, I would already be dead."

Not sure she believed him but seeing the pleading look in Eurie's eyes, Izzie turned toward a door that would lead her from the room. "I may be leaving the room, but I promise you, I will be listening. I am going into the kitchen where there are plenty of sharp knives. Do not underestimate me. If I feel that you are a threat to my brother, I will not hesitate to use them." With that said, she exited the room, slamming the door shut.

Eurie turned toward Cap and Smitty. "What are you doing here? Apollo's men are still mad that you shot him," said Eurie.

"We need your help," said Cap.

"I cannot help you. If they even find out I am talking to you, they will kill me," said Eurie.

"Well then, let's not let them find out, but you are going to help me. Or I will make it known you made a deal for your life when Apollo was shot," responded Cap.

Knowing that Cap was serious, Eurie responded, "What do you need?"

"I need to know who Apollo sold the female soldier to," answered Cap.

"He said her to the African," replied Eurie.

"He lied. He sold all the men to the warlord, but not the girl," said Cap, reaching out to grab Eurie by the arm. "And I need to know where she is, right now," he added with a squeeze on his arm.

Cap usually exhibited more finesse, but the past few days had stretched his patience just about as far as he could take. Lines of strain had caused deep grooves to form around his mouth, and his cheeks looked as sharp as razors. As far as he was concerned, he didn't have time to fool around with Eurie's sensitivities. He needed answers now; time was ticking, and God only knew what was happening to McBeth during the seconds he was having to play tootsie with Eurie.

"Eurie," Cap tried to sound civil, "you owe us."

Eurie grimaced and said, "Okay, I will find out. I have all his paperwork in my office at the shop, but you two cannot go there."

"Go get it. We will wait here, and if you double-cross us, there will be nowhere for you to hide," said Smitty.

At that moment, Izzie opened the door and walked up to Eurie. "Selling people. You fool… How could you…" she started but stopped when she saw the look on Eurie's face. She knew him; he wasn't a bad man, just a weak one. All their lives, she had been cleaning up after him.

"Go ahead," she ordered him. "You get those papers. I'll entertain your guests while you are gone." She walked over to a large coat stand and removed a black raincoat from a hook. Giving it to Eurie, she patted the collar around his face. "Take an umbrella and hurry. With this downpour, your chances of getting back safe are greatly increased." She turned away from her brother and went back into the kitchen.

Eurie put on his raincoat and headed out the door. "This is my last favor. After this, we are even," he said, closing the door.

Eurie's sister came back out of the kitchen. She pointed to the living room and said, "You might as well make yourselves comfortable. I'll get you some coffee."

Cap and Smitty went into the living room and sat down on a flowery sofa piled with pillows. It was obvious the couch was chosen for decor and not comfort, and both found themselves sitting stiffly on the edge of it. Eurie's sister returned with two black coffees and a bottle of cognac.

"Please help yourselves. I am going to go up to my bedroom and watch for my brother to return. If you need anything else, it is in the kitchen," she said as she attempted to back out of the room.

Cap stood up and approached her. "I think it best if you stay with us."

"Why?" she asked. "Are you afraid that I might knife you? If I were going to do that, I would have already. I just happen to hate human traffickers, and it sickens me to think my brother might have been in league with them." She turned toward the door again. "I am going upstairs. You can try to stop me if you want, but I promise you won't walk away from such an attempt unscathed." She stared at the two men and then resumed walking.

Smitty found himself grinning as Cap just watched her walk away. "Do you really think she is going to do anything that might get her brother hurt?" Cap shook his head, and Smitty continued, "Let her go. Come have some coffee and maybe a little cognac. I don't know about you, but I am damned cold."

"I hope Eurie doesn't try anything funny," said Cap as he walked toward a chair in the room. Seeing that Cap wasn't going to sit back on the couch, Smitty got up.

"Me too. I think I'm going to slip out the back door and watch for him," said Smitty. He went back through the house and exited through the rear door.

Thirty minutes passed, and finally, the front door opened. Eurie had returned alone. As he was closing the door, Smitty walked up behind him and entered the house with him.

Wasting no time, Cap asked, "Did you find her?"

"Yes, she was sold to Kim Su Dux in North Korea," answered Eurie.

"North Korea! Who the hell is that?" said Cap.

"He's a broker that resells women to clients in the China and Russian area," answered Eurie.

"Are you sure?" asked Smitty.

"Absolutely positive," replied Eurie. He took off his raincoat and rehung it on the tree stand.

"Where is he located in North Korea?" asked Cap.

Eurie pulled out a piece of paper and read the location. "He is in Tumangang, North Korea, and she was sold for one hundred thousand US dollars," he read out loud.

"You better be telling us the truth, or we will be back," said Smitty.

"It's the truth, and I don't want you to come back. Please leave now before someone sees you," said Eurie, opening his front door.

"Be seeing you, Eurie," said Smitty as they disappeared in the pouring rain.

"Signal the master chief. We are ready for pickup," said Cap as they walked toward the port area.

They approached the front gate and waited on the side obscured by abandoned vehicles. They sat poised to move. A large truck and trailer pulled up to the gate. On the back of the trailer was a bright-red shipping container.

"Let's hitch a ride," said Cap, sliding under the trailer and grabbing hold of a support bar.

Smitty followed and did the same. As the truck started pulling out, the two men pulled themselves up so that their bodies couldn't be seen by any observer. Just inside the gates, they saw their barge, and as the truck moved slowly around a bend, the two dropped down and rolled out from under the trailer. They got on their feet and sprinted to the barge. Onboard, they took off their coats and put their wet suits on. Cap crawled down the ladder first and pulled the rope with their gear on the other end. Cap slipped into the water first then Smitty. They donned their mouthpieces and disappeared under the dark waters of the port.

The two men swam out from the pier and looked for the mini sub. It was only seconds before they saw their ride. They swam under the sub, and the hatch slowly opened. Both men entered the sub and sat down on the bench. Slowly the door closed, and the water exited the chamber. When the water was below their waist, they removed their masks and tanks. Eventually, all the water had cleared the chamber, and the door opened.

"What's the good word, gentlemen?" asked the master chief.

"We know where she is, but it's North Korea," said Smitty.

"North Korea!" yelled the master chief. "What the Sam's hell do they want with her?"

"Not sure, but we are going to get her," said Cap.

The master chief returned to the sub's controls, and they headed back to the ship. No one spoke the entire trip back.

Eventually, the sub was raised out of the water, and all four men exited.

"What now?" asked the master chief.

"Back to our team to plan a rescue," said Cap bluntly.

"You know our government will definitely sit this one out, going to North Korea," said the master chief. "But if you need any help, I could use a little vacation," he said, shaking Cap's hand.

"Thank you, Master Chief," said Cap, walking to the C-2.

"Great seeing you, Smitty. You guys stay safe, and you have my number," added the master chief.

"We will, and thank you for the sub ride," said Smitty, shaking his pal's hand.

Smitty entered the plane waiting on the deck to find Cap was talking to the pilots.

"They can have us back to base in a few hours. As soon as we hit the ground, I want to get the team together and look at our options," said Cap.

"You got it, buddy," said Smitty as the guys strapped into their harnesses.

"Get ready for the slingshot then straight home," said the copilot.

The pilot received permission to take off, and with a snap, the C-2 was airborne, headed back to base.

CHAPTER 13

HOMECOMING

The bright-pink C-130 was approaching Russian airspace soon after its takeoff from Yokosuka, Japan. Michelena radioed she was having a fuel issue and requested to land at a small airstrip in Khasan, a small providence located near the Russian, Chinese, and North Korean borders. Knowing they would have to convince the Russians they had a fuel problem, Cap had placed a solenoid cell on the fuel line so that the fuel would be unable to flow.

After a little persuading and some unknown help from a certain Russian government official, the plane was granted permission to land.

Dropping down from twenty thousand feet, the plane headed toward the short runway. Inside the plane, the team readied their equipment. The plan was to open the rear hatch while landing; and when the plane was at the end of the runway, before she made her turn back to the terminal area, the team would slip out in the dense foliage that surrounded the old airport.

"Cap, we're at ten thousand feet. I can't open the door until right before touchdown, but it's going to be a bumpy as hell ride for you guys," said Michelena.

"We understand," said Cap as he turned to tell the team the situation.

"Everyone, strap down your equipment and make sure you are ready to roll when we get the green light. Amir, you stick close to Smitty. We can't be seen, so you will have to move fast to the tree line," he added. Since the team was unsure in what condition McBeth or the girls might be in, they had brought the doctor with them. He had proofed himself to be capable in their earlier skirmishes.

"I love a hundred-yard dash in full gear," said Smitty, trying to make everyone smile.

They all knew what was at stake if they were seen or, worse, caught.

The plane dropped lower toward the airstrip.

"Cap, I think we may have a little luck on our side. It's raining," said Michelena.

"That will help," said Cap.

"Okay, guys, runway in sight, and I'm starting our approached. Standby for green," said Callie from the copilot seat.

"Guys, if you think we are compromised and are seen, take off immediately and get to international airspace, understand?" said Cap to Michelena and Callie.

They both nodded yes and went back to the landing procedures.

The landing gear lowered, and the rear hatch started to come down. This made landing ten times harder for the pilots, but the girls had practiced it many times for cases just like these. The wind was whipping through the plane like a tornado, and the team was holding on to their safety straps with all their might.

The plane touched down with a hard thud, and the rear hatch opened a little more. The pilots had to make sure the door didn't completely open because it would touch the ground and warn any observer that the rear door was open. The plane now rolled on the ground, near the turnaround point on the runway. As the plane started to make its turn, Callie signaled the green light to the team, who were staged at the top of the ramp. When the plane turned slowly, the team was able to exit the plane, maintain their balance, and start running for the tree line.

Cap, being the last man out, signaled to Callie, and she closed the rear hatch. From an observer's view, the plane just made a slow turn and taxied down the runway to the terminal, where they were met with official government vehicles.

Once the plane stopped, they were completely surrounded by airport and military vehicles.

"Let's hope the little mechanical story holds up, and the fuel issue is handled quick," said Michelena.

"I sure hope so. Without their support, there's no quick takeoff in our immediate future," said Callie as she opened the door and was met by several soldiers waiting outside.

"Hey, guys, thank you so much to coming to our aid," she said.

Callie was on her best behavior. Before leaving for Russia, she and Michelena had carefully prepared with the idea of distracting any soldiers who came to check out the aircraft. Even their makeup had been applied with the idea of quietly seducing the Russians, and looking at the two women, the soldiers never suspected they were being deceived by the two women.

The soldiers were taken back to see the two pilots were women, who were in their customary pink jumpsuits, which always brought attention to them.

"Which one of you boys is going to cure my problems?" said Michelena to the red-faced soldiers. She leaned into the men as she uttered the request.

"Ladies, my name is Andre, and I am the administrator of this airport," said a short, stubby man, pushing his way past the soldiers.

"I was told to give you ladies all the assistance you needed to repair your plane and get you back in the air as soon as possible. I guess you have a lot of friends in high places," he said with a smirk.

"Why, thank you, Andre," said Michelena. She moved closer to the small man and gently placed her hand on his forehead. Once her hand was there, she nonchalantly rubbed her fingers across his receding hairline, almost throwing up in the process.

"Which of these guys are mechanics?" Callie asked, getting straight to the point. It seemed to her that she and Michelena didn't need to play any more charades with the soldiers; their Russian friend had already smoothed things out for them.

Andre motioned for two men that were standing at the rear of the small crowd that had developed. They made their way to him.

"These men can fix anything," said Andre.

"Great, let me show you the way," said Callie as she turned to lead the men.

"Just one minute, young lady," said Andre

Callie turned, expecting to hear their maneuver had been observed.

"These men know your plane inside and out. I need you to join your friend and myself in the lounge until the repairs are made," said Andre.

"Is there a problem, Andre?" asked Michelena. Her voice purred the question.

"No, dear, no problem, but since you are guest of my country, I have to keep you with me all the time," he added.

"All the time," said Michelena.

"Yes," said Andre.

"And I hope it takes a while so we can get to know each other," he added, taking her arm and leading her toward the building, with Callie following.

"Looks like the girls are okay," said Smitty from the tree line.

"Okay, let's hump it to the lake and set up the crossing," said Cap.

The team's plan was to follow the Russian Chinese border northeast for about five klicks until they made it to Lake Khasan. At Lake Khasan, they would turn south and travel for two klicks, crossing into China. About a klick away was the Tumen River. On the other side of the river was North Korea. The team carried inflatable rafts and planned to set them in the water just east of a shoe factory located on the river. There they would cross the river into North Korea and go about two klicks south to Tumangang.

The team made good time, covering the seven klicks in about an hour since they kept their pace at a steady half-jog. For that hour, everything seemed fine. Wearing camouflage, they blended into the scenery; however, when they met the shoe factory, they were met with heavy security.

"Guys, we need to move our insertion into the river a little further north," said Smitty. "It will mean a little more paddling, but the current will be with us, so it shouldn't take too much longer."

"I sure hope we don't run into any patrols. Not having any motors and just paddling won't let us outrun anyone," said Murph.

"We're lucky the river isn't that wide here, and we have a great line of sight in both directions to see and approaching patrols," said Cap. "It's almost sunset, so let's get these boats in position."

The plan was to wait until sunset to cross the river. They would then use the darkness to hide their approach on the river and to conceal themselves for the half a klick of open ground they had to cover on the other side.

Cap waited until the time was right to start the approach.

"Okay, guys, let's roll," he said.

The team had already inflated the three rafts they brought with them. They silently slid the rafts into the water, and the current immediately started pushing the boats down the river. The only thing stronger than the current was the terrible stench that came from the river. Decades of pollution and runoff from the factories located up and down the Tumen River had created a soupy mess for the rafts to traverse.

Since the rafts were connected by ropes, they stayed close to each other. The rain that had fallen earlier in the day had disappeared. In quiet and solemn thought, the guys paddled hard to cross the river, fighting the current that threatened to push them past their desired landing point.

Two thirds across the river, Cap motioned for the guys to step up the paddling.

"We need to be at this position to avoid being seen by sentries," said Cap as he used his laser to point out the landing spot. The laser could only be seen if someone was wearing the NVG like the team had.

The team neared the desired spot, and Cap said," Okay, guys, deflate your rafts so we can move quick once on shore."

The team members slid into the cold water. They were about fifty feet from shore, but they were able to touch the river bottom. The rafts deflated and were rolled up into their carrying packs. Silently the team worked their way toward shore, staying low in the water so they didn't silhouette themselves to observers at a distance.

Cap signaled for the team to stop and get low in the water. Dim headlights from an approaching vehicle shone out onto the silt/dirt-filled shoreline. The six-wheeled military vehicle passed by on the shoreline and never slowed. The team slowly raised out of the water and sprinted across the open shoreline to a small rock structure near the tree line.

The team concealed the rafts and stowed away their water gear. Cap pulled out his map, and the team gathered for a last look at it. Secured in a waterproof container, the map was dry. He signaled for Smitty to shine a flashlight on the map.

"We are here," Cap said as he placed his finger on the map. He then pointed to a larger building, about one hundred yards away. "There is no cover between here and there, so we have to remain concealed."

"After that building, we have another three hundred yards to get to the target location," added Smitty.

"I need one man to stay with the gear. The last thing we need is to find someone at our hiding place or the gear missing if we are being chased," said Cap.

"I'll stay, and you can take Coop," volunteered Bruce.

With nothing more to say, the nine men moved as one as they worked their way to the first building. There they plotted a course to the target location.

"Smitty, take six guys in three two men teams and set up a perimeter. Have one team cut the power on my mark. When you are set, we will make our approach," said Cap.

Smitty nodded and tapped MK, Snyder, and Miller on the shoulder. "You guys with me. Lieutenant, you and Bain cut the power and head back here to watch for stragglers," he said, and the two men disappeared into the darkness.

Smitty gathered the remaining men. "Snyder, you and Miller work your way to the rear as soon as Cap gives us the green light," he said, pointing to the dim lit area south of the team.

"Amir, you, Murph, and Cooper are with me. We are going to the front door," said Cap.

Smitty and MK worked their way around the building but stopped short. "Guys, I got four guards on the east side of the building," he said as all the team members froze in their positions. "It looks like maybe a smoke break, and they are splitting up. Snyder, you got two headed your way."

"Copy that, but I got two guards coming around from the west side as we speak," said Snyder.

"Looks like three-two men teams working the perimeter," said Smitty.

"We need to get past these guys, but we need to be silent," said Cap.

"I'll get in position to intercept the guards moving west. Smitty, get ready to take out the two guards near you, and Snyder, you guys get ready too," said Cap. "We need to do this all at the same time."

The three teams moved in on the guards. One by one, they confirmed they were in place. They waited until the moving guards approached Cap's position. "Silently," said Cap, almost whispering on the radio.

Smitty acknowledged and slid his knife out of its sleeve.

"On my mark," said Cap.

"Three, two, one, go," said Cap, and the team moved.

Silently and stealthily, the guys moved up behind the unsuspecting guards. Smitty and MK simultaneously grabbed the guards with one hand over their mouths and slit their throats, dragging their lifeless bodies to a covered area so no one passing by would see them. The other two teams followed the same procedure.

Once clear, Cap began speaking, "Smitty, move your guys into position. Miller and Bain, let's set up for our entry."

All team members moved to their assigned position. Cap, Amir, Murph, and Coop set up to make entry.

"Bain, cut the power!" said Cap as the entry team lowered their NVGs.

Lieutenant cut the power, and the guys went in.

The team entered two by two, clearing the rooms on the left and right as they passed. The first couple rooms were unoccupied. The third room was the barracks. Cap, Murph, and Coop entered the room while Amir covered the hallway. The fireworks started immediately, but the team took the guards by surprise and were able to take the seven guards out. Amir dispatched a couple that stuck their heads out into the hallway to see what the commotions in the barracks were about. There still was half the building to clear. And by now, the building was buzzing with guards running back and forth in the dark.

Cap motioned for the team to press on. They maintained radio silence and used hand signals to communicate. They entered the radio room and took out the radio operator then disabled the radio. They came to a heavily locked door, and Cap called Murph up to breach the door. Slinging his rifle, Murph pulled a sawed-off shotgun out for the job.

"So much for staying quiet," said Cap as he motioned for Murph to take down the door.

Three shots each to the door hinges did the trick, and the door was open. Inside the room, the team was met with screams from the girls. Five girls were sitting up on narrow beds, and one female was strapped to a chair in the middle of the room with a black hood over her head.

The men went to freeing the girls and spoke to them gently.

"We are here to help you," said Coop.

"Calm down, ladies. We don't need to bring all the guards in on us," said Murph. Of course, that statement was ridiculous with all the commotion going on.

Cap walked over to the woman in the chair and took off her hood. He was greeted with a familiar smile.

"Good to see you, Cap. What took you so long?" said McBeth.

"Traffic," responded Cap as he cut her loose. "Can you stand?"

"Hell yes, but I need to know if there are any other girls in this camp," she said.

"If you're looking for Beth, she's safe at home, waiting on you," said Cap as McBeth hugged him with tears in her eyes.

"Thank you," she said.

"You're welcome, but let's have this conversation when we are on our way home, okay," he said.

Amir was firing a few rounds down the hallway and turned to Cap. "I think we need to get moving, Boss," he said, turning to see him hugged up with McBeth.

The team had freed all the girls, but Cindy was standing in the middle of the room, emotionless.

Murph walked the first girl to the door. "This is Amir. I want you to grab hold of his belt and don't let go, no matter what. Do you understand?" he asked the girl, and she nodded yes.

He then took the second girl and said, "I want you to hold onto Coop's shirt and follow him. Now don't let go."

The young girl just whimpered, "Okay."

"Cap, we will keep the other three girls between us, and I'll take up the rear," Murph said to Cap.

"That's cool. You two ladies, hold hands, and you, young lady, keep a tight grip on my belt," he said, pointing to the blue-eyed brunette.

The first two girls held hands, but Cindy was still standing there, unwilling to even move. The girl closest to her reached out and grabbed her hand as the group started its exit. At first, Cindy resisted, but once Murph, who was behind Cindy, pushed, she began to move out of the room.

Gunfire erupted at the back of the group. Amir, who was in front, knew Murph was fighting off guards at the rear, so he pushed hard to get the group back to the same door they entered. He slowed down only at the barrack door to make sure no other guards were in there since their last visit. Amir and his partner passed through Murph. McBeth along with Coop and his partner passed him by, but as Cap started, shots hit the doorframe from inside the room. Now the team was held up with half on each side of the door.

"McBeth, you and Coop take the two girls and go out into the courtyard," said Cap.

"Smitty, I have a package coming out the door. Cover the girls and secure them. We have a little setback, but I will be right out," said Cap.

"Copy that," said Smitty.

McBeth and Coop with the first two girls headed to the door.

"Amir, you and I are going to lay down suppression fire and get these girls across the doorway," said Cap as he positioned himself.

Amir assumed the same position on the other side of the doorway.

"Now," said Cap, and the two men started firing into the room.

Murph knew the drill and pushed the first girl across the doorway to safety before returning for the next. Again, Cap and Amir started firing, and Murph moved the second girl, leaving Cindy standing behind Cap. Murph moved back to get Cindy but was met with two rounds to his chest. Guards had regrouped and were moving down the hallway from the back of the building. Cap turned and opened on the guards moving toward them and in one motion pulled Cindy to the ground and stood over her and his injured friend.

"Get those girls out of here," said Cap to Amir. "Now!"

Amir nodded yes, but before he moved, he tossed a grenade into the room.

"Heads up, Cap, just giving you a little breathing room."

Outside the explosion blew the window out.

"They must be in a bunch of trouble to risk making that kind of noise," said Smitty, pushing McBeth and the girls toward the tree line.

"I need to go back," said McBeth.

"There's nothing you can do at this point, except get my ass kicked by Cap for letting you go back," he replied. "Even so, have you looked at yourself recently? The flesh is hanging on your bones, and I know you think you can help, but I promise you—and you know I'm telling the truth—you would only distract Cap."

McBeth took a deep breath and coughed. She knew she was in bad shape, but this was Cap who needed help. However, Smitty was right; she was more of a liability than help.

Meanwhile, back inside, Cap looked down at Cindy and asked, "Is he breathing?"

"Hell, yes, I'm breathing," responded Murph.

Cindy started crying and mumbling, seemed she was coming out of her catatonic state, "I can't go home to my family after this."

"It's going to be okay, young lady," said Murph. He was getting up on one knee to help Cap keep the guards pinned in the rooms down the hallway—seemed his bulletproof vest had protected him from the bullets. "God, it hurts to breathe," he muttered under his breath. "I hate these things."

Cap took a minute to look at his friend. "Murph, I'm about ready to change mags. Are you ready?"

"Yes, sir," he said and started firing down the hallway. He was trained to ignore the pain until after the conflict.

The constant firing kept the guards from sticking their heads out into a dark hallway, not knowing where the shots were coming from.

Cap said, "I reloaded. We need to work our way to the door."

Cindy was becoming hysterical. It seemed the thought of being rescued was worse than being held in the camp.

When Murph and Cindy stood up, Murph reached his hands out and said to Cindy. "Give me your hand, and I will take you home."

Cindy reached out for Murph's hand but instead dropped something in each. She then turned and ran back down the hallway so fast neither man had a chance to grab her. Luckily, they didn't. Murph looked down in his hands, and he had two hand grenade pins. Cindy had pulled the grenades off his vest when they were on the ground, and now she was running back into hell with two grenades in her hands.

"Cap, get down," he said as he grabbed Cap's vest and pulled him backward.

The explosion destroyed the rooms the guards were hiding in.

While the noise was ringing in their ears, the two men stood up and started running toward the door. They hit the courtyard and were in a full sprint when they met up with the others.

"You guys okay?" asked Amir. Although he asked both guys, his attention was on Murph. "I saw you hit in the chest twice."

Murph just shrugged and patted his chest. "Lucky body armor. I never leave home without it."

"Yes, but—" That's as far as Amir got when McBeth interrupted.

"Where's Cindy?" she asked.

Cap shook his head and said, "She didn't make it. I know what happened here, but the thought of going home terrified her."

"Dammit!" yelled McBeth.

"We need to move before any more guards or soldiers show up," said Smitty.

The team ran as fast as they could to get back to where they had hidden their inflatable rafts. The return trip was slowed by the girls, and even though McBeth was normally a fast sprinter, it was obvious she was hurting. Still, within a few minutes longer, they were back at their debarkation site. The group spilt up among the three boats and were quickly on their way downstream.

"We have to be on the other shoreline before we reach the bridge," said Cap.

There was a bridge that crossed the Tumen River; the east side was North Korea, and the west side was Russia.

"If we get caught, I want it to be on the Russian side," he said to the team as they paddled across the river.

It took them about ten minutes to reach the Russian shoreline. The bridge was in sight, but the darkness helped conceal them. The team beached the rafts, not bothering to deflate them, and ran to the tree line.

"We are about a klick away from the airport," said Cap, "and we need to move fast."

"I'll signal Callie when we are in position. By now, the fuel line should have been repaired and the plane refueled," said Smitty.

The plane's fuel lines had been rigged with a remote solenoid that stopped the flow of fuel. Once Callie knew the team was ready, she could trigger the solenoid, and the Russian mechanic could take credit for fixing the plane.

All was moving well, until the headlights came on.

"No one move and drop your weapons," came the Russian voice over the speakers.

The group was caught.

Back at the airport, Andre and the girls were sitting and talking about fashion and how much the world had changed in the past few years. Andre's cell phone rang. He spoke then started just bobbing his head yes to the voice on the phone. He hung up and just looked at the girls.

"Follow me," he said in a not-so-friendly voice.

"Is our plane fixed?" asked Callie, knowing it wasn't.

"Just be quiet and follow me," he said again.

Andre led the girls outside to a hangar near the main building. The doors opened, and sitting in a semicircle in the floor was the team, plus the rescued girls. Michelena and Callie didn't know how to respond; they just looked at Andre.

"Well, it seems your job was to distract me while you US Soldiers invaded my country," he said to Michelena

"It's not like that, Andre," she said. "These girls were being held in North Korea, and we had to get them out," she continued.

"North Korea," said Andre in a loud voice.

"There's going to be hell to pay, and they will think it is us who invaded them," he said, shaking his head. "I will have to hand you over to them just to keep the peace."

Everyone's head was lowered and shaking in disbelief. They had gotten so far to fail now.

"Okay, everyone, back into the transport van," said Andre.

Cap knew the guys were thinking about how to overpower the guards, but he knew they wouldn't risk any harm to the girls. They would have to pick a time during transport to make their move.

"Oh, you two, stay here with me," said Andre to Michelena and Callie as the transport van door closed in front of them. "My mechanic found your remote switch and removed it. He figured that was your problem since the fuel flowed perfectly with it gone."

"What are you going to do with us?" asked Callie.

Instead of responding, he just directed the girls to follow him as he walked out of the hangar.

The girls stopped when they heard the plane engines start.

"What are you going to do with our plane?" asked Michelena.

The rear hatch opened, and the transport van drove up into the plane. The girls turned and looked at Andre.

"Friend in high places," he said with a smile.

Both girls kissed his cheeks and ran toward the plane.

Inside the airplane, guards had left the van unattended. The guys inside didn't know what was happening until Callie opened the door and told everyone to get out and strap themselves in for the flight home.

"What's going on?" said Cap.

Callie just responded. "Mich and I just made a new friend," and they laughed.

The plane taxied down the runway, and Michelena radioed to traffic control, asking permission to take off.

Andre responded on the radio. "Permission granted, but I would hook an immediate left and not go near Korean airspace," he said with a chuckle.

"Copy that, my friend, and I hope to see you again soon," she said.

Cap had joined Michelena in the cockpit while Callie helped with the girls. Amir was looking at Murph's injuries.

"Lucky you had that extra plate in the front of your vest," said Amir, tapping the plate next to the two bullet hits.

"Hang around me, Doc, and you won't have anything to ever worry about," said Murph.

Callie went over to McBeth and said, "I'm sorry about your friend. Murph said she was too terrified to come home with us."

"She was so mistreated by the guards. I kept trying to reassure her it would be okay that someone would come get us," said McBeth. "But I think she was beyond our help. Sometimes she retreated so far into herself I feared she had disappeared. Seems to me she got her final revenge when she threw those grenades."

Callie placed a blanket over McBeth's shoulders and said, "As long as you hold onto hope, you can survive and use your experience to make a difference to others."

McBeth looked at Callie like she had seen a ghost.

"That's the second time in my life someone has said that to me. The other time was when I was a little girl and my family had died. Where did you get that from?" she said, sitting up in her seat.

Callie just pointed at Cap, who looked back at McBeth and smiled.

The End

ABOUT THE AUTHOR

DM Gaither authored this action-packed title on the heels of a thirty-year public-service career. He explored firsthand the intricacies of the relationship between governments and private contractors. His stint as a private contractor was preceded by a healthy career as a police officer and a SWAT operator.